Hartwell James

Military Heroes of the United States

From Lexington to Santiago

Hartwell James

Military Heroes of the United States
From Lexington to Santiago

ISBN/EAN: 9783337194413

Printed in Europe, USA, Canada, Australia, Japan

Cover: Foto ©Andreas Hilbeck / pixelio.de

More available books at **www.hansebooks.com**

Military Heroes, U. S.

Assassination of Colonel Ellsworth.

ALTEMUS' YOUNG PEOPLE'S LIBRARY

MILITARY HEROES

OF THE

UNITED STATES

FROM LEXINGTON TO SANTIAGO

BY

HARTWELL JAMES

WITH NINETY-FOUR ILLUSTRATIONS

PHILADELPHIA
HENRY ALTEMUS

IN UNIFORM STYLE

Copiously Illustrated

THE PILGRIM'S PROGRESS
ALICE'S ADVENTURES IN WONDERLAND
THROUGH THE LOOKING-GLASS & WHAT ALICE FOUND THERE
ROBINSON CRUSOE
THE CHILD'S STORY OF THE BIBLE
THE CHILD'S LIFE OF CHRIST
LIVES OF THE PRESIDENTS OF THE UNITED STATES
THE SWISS FAMILY ROBINSON
THE FABLES OF ÆSOP
CHRISTOPHER COLUMBUS AND THE DISCOVERY OF AMERICA
MOTHER GOOSE'S RHYMES, JINGLES AND FAIRY TALES
EXPLORATION AND ADVENTURE IN THE FROZEN SEAS
THE STORY OF DISCOVERY AND EXPLORATION IN AFRICA
GULLIVER'S TRAVELS
ARABIAN NIGHTS' ENTERTAINMENTS
WOOD'S NATURAL HISTORY
A CHILD'S HISTORY OF ENGLAND, by CHARLES DICKENS
BLACK BEAUTY, by ANNA SEWELL
ANDERSEN'S FAIRY TALES
GRIMM'S FAIRY TALES
GRANDFATHER'S CHAIR, by NATHANIEL HAWTHORNE
FLOWER FABLES, by LOUISA M. ALCOTT
AUNT MARTHA'S CORNER CUPBOARD
WATER-BABIES, by CHARLES KINGSLEY
BATTLES OF THE WAR FOR INDEPENDENCE
BATTLES OF THE WAR FOR THE UNION
YOUNG PEOPLE'S HISTORY OF SPANISH WAR
HEROES OF THE UNITED STATES NAVY
HEROES OF THE UNITED STATES ARMY

Price 50 Cents Each

HENRY ALTEMUS, PHILADELPHIA

CONTENTS.

iv.   *Contents.*

INTRODUCTORY.

NO apology is necessary for a series of sketches portraying intelligent military heroism. It is right that we acclaim our heroes, and tell the stories of their lives by our firesides.

Heroic traditions make heroic nations, and while it does not follow that those who handled the bayonet, swung the sabre, or sent the pitiless shell into opposing ranks at Gettysburg were emulating the deeds of their Fathers in the days of the Revolution, or that those who swarmed up the hills and through the ingenious entanglements of the Spanish defenses at San Juan and El Caney were consciously stimulated by the traditions of the Civil War; yet the love of country and humanity was there and set the fighting string twanging in the breast, and nerved the arm to deeds of irresistible valor.

The lives of the commanding figures that are shown on the pages of American military history are worthy of emulation. From Lexington to Santiago the story is the same —the record is splendid.

MILITARY HEROES
OF THE UNITED STATES.

MASSACHUSETTS was the soul of the movement that led to the revolt of the English provinces in America, and the first appeal to arms between the colonists and the mother country took place upon her soil. George III. was King, and General Gage occupied the city of Boston with a British army in the year 1775. Both sides were making preparations for the coming strife. A "Committee of Supplies" had gathered military stores at Concord, and learning of this, Gage sent a detachment of about eight hundred men to destroy them, on the night of

April 18; but information of the movement had reached
the Committee, and Dr. Joseph Warren despatched William Dawes through Roxbury and Paul Revere by way of
Charlestown to Lexington. Revere was stopped by two

British officers, but being mounted on a fine horse he escaped. As he rode through Medford he aroused the cap-
tains of the minute-men, and stopping at almost every house
on his way to Lexington, aroused the inhabitants and
spread the news. Dawes also reached Lexington in safety.

Paul Revere's Midnight Ride.

PAUL REVERE.

THIS American patriot was born on January 1, 1735, in the city of Boston. His occupation was that of a goldsmith, but he learned the art of engraving on copper, and in 1775 engraved and printed the paper money ordered by Congress. He was one of the band who threw the tea overboard in Boston harbor. He died in Boston, May 10, 1818, at the age of eighty-three years. Longfellow immortalized him in a stirring poem entitled " Paul Revere's Ride."

Samuel Prescott spread the alarm from Lexington to Concord, and about two o'clock in the morning the alarm bell on the belfry in the meeting-house brought together the inhabitants, young and old, with their firelocks. Messengers were sent to other villages, and stores and provisions were hurried away and secreted in the woods.

At Lexington, at about the same hour, the village green was thronged with excited men. The aged stood shoulder to shoulder with their sons, and by their example and experience gave encouragement and strength to the undisciplined mass. One hundred and thirty men had answered to their names. Captain John Parker, their commander, had ordered each piece loaded with powder and ball; but the men were instructed not to be the first to fire. No signs of the approach of the enemy being visible, they were dismissed with orders to reassemble at the roll of the drum.

Battle of Lexington.

The foremost party of the British came in sight about eleven o'clock in the forenoon of April 19, led by Major Pitcairn. Knowing that their errand was discovered, six companies of light infantry were despatched to Concord to secure the two bridges over the river, and messengers were sent to Boston for reinforcements. As the drums beat the alarm, about seventy men assembled on the village green, nearly half of whom were without arms. Captain Parker ordered them to go to the meeting-house and equip themselves and then join the company. Thirty-eight men who were armed he formed into line, in single file, at the north end of the green. Before those who were in the meeting-house could equip themselves. Pitcairn's men came up and cut them off from the little band under Parker. Pitcairn marched his men to about fifty feet from the handful of patriots, and then, brandishing his sword, he shouted: "Disperse, you villains! Lay down your arms! Why don't you disperse, you rebels? Disperse!" The patriots stood their ground, and then Pitcairn gave the order to " Fire!" The order was followed first by a few guns, which did no execution, and then by a close and deadly discharge of musketry. In the disparity of numbers, Parker ordered every man to take care of himself, and they accordingly dispersed. While doing so, the second platoon of the enemy fired, killing several and wounding others. Then, and not till, then, did a few of the patriots, on their own impulse, return the British fire. These random shots of fugitives or dying men did no harm. Seven of the patriots were killed and nine wounded. One who was taken prisoner was shot in his endeavor to escape. Thus the first skirmish for liberty was fought.

The British pushed on to Concord and destroyed the
stores. The liberty-pole and several gun-carriages were
burned; the court-house took fire, but the fire was extinguished. By this time some four hundred patriots had
gathered on the rising ground above Concord bridge.
"Will you let them burn down the town?" cried one.
Taking counsel together, the entire body resolved "To
march into the middle of the town for its defense, or die
in the attempt." Colonel Barrett, who was in command,
gave orders to advance, but not to fire unless attacked.
"I have not a man that is afraid to go," said Isaac Davis,
of Acton, and drawing his sword, he cried: "March!" At
the head of his men he led the way to the bridge, with
Major Buttrick, of Concord, by his side, followed by the
minute-men and militia. The British began to take up
the planks; to prevent it the patriots quickened their steps.
At this the British fired one or two shots up the river;
then another, by which two were wounded. A volley followed, and Isaac Davis and Abner Hosmer fell dead. Then
Major Buttrick gave the order, "Fire, fellow soldiers; for
God's sake, fire!" and a general discharge from the whole
line of patriots was given, several of the enemy, including
three lieutenants, falling on the spot. In two minutes all
was hushed. The British retreated in disorder towards
their main body; the countrymen were left in possession of
the bridge.

At this world-renowned Battle of Concord the patriots
acted from impulse, and at first attempted no pursuit, but
as the British forces retreated the militia ran over the lines
and ambushed the flying troops. Every piece of woods,
every rock by the wayside, served as a lurking place. The

hills seemed to the British to swarm with "rebels" as
an unintermitted fire was poured on them from behind
stone walls and trees. The British began to run rather
than retreat in order. Their officers vainly tried to stop
their flight, for they were being driven before the Americans like sheep. About two o'clock in the afternoon reinforcements met them, and forming into a square enclosed
the fugitives, who lay down for rest on the ground, "their
tongues hanging out of their mouths like those of dogs
after a chase." After a rest of half an hour the British
resumed their retreat, but the patriots dogged every step
and finally drove them under the guns of the ships-of-war
in the harbor of Boston.

After Lexington and Concord the militia hurried to
Boston. As their terms of service expired other troops
were enlisted. There was great want of money, clothing
and ammunition. The Committee of Safety decided " That
Bunker's Hill be maintained by sufficient force being
posted there," and on the night of June 16, 1775, about
one thousand men, under the command of Colonel William
Prescott, assembled on Cambridge Common. After a
prayer by President Langdon, of Harvard College, the
troops marched to Breed's Hill, "as being the more commanding site," and there entrenchments were thrown up;
yet the memorable engagement that followed will always
be known as the Battle of Bunker Hill. So rapidly did
the patriots ply their entrenching tools through the hot
night that by daylight the breastworks "assumed form and
height and capacity for defense."

About three o'clock, on June 17, the British troops
advanced to the assault. Twice the patriots' terrible fire

Death of Isaac Davis.

drove them back in confusion, but their ammunition gave out, and after the third attack they were obliged to retreat

Death of Major Pitcairn.

across Charlestown neck. The slaughter among the British was terrific. Among those shot down was Major Pit-

Retreat of the British from Concord.

cairn, who had ordered the " rebels " to disperse at Lexington. " Nothing," wrote a British officer, " could be
more shocking than the carnage that followed the storming
of this work. We tumbled over the dead to get at the
living, who were crowding out of the gorge of the redoubt

Prescott's Men in the Redoubt.

in order to form under the defenses which they had prepared to cover their retreat." Before the British attacked,
the tall form of Prescott was seen walking leisurely along
the parapet to inspire his men. General Gage, in Boston,
by the aid of a glass, could plainly see his commanding

figure, and turning to Counselor Willard, who stood near him, asked who it was. Willard, recognizing his brother-in-law, said: "That is Colonel Prescott." "Will he fight?" inquired Gage. "Yes, sir," replied Willard; "he is an old soldier, and will fight as long as a drop of blood remains in his veins." "The works must be carried immediately," responded Gage, as he turned upon his heel to give orders.

Prescott was the last to leave the fort. Though his coat and waistcoat were pierced with bayonet-thrusts, which he parried with his sword, he got off unhurt. Among the killed was Dr. Joseph Warren, one of the most active and distinguished of the patriots.

JOSEPH WARREN.

JOSEPH WARREN was born on July 11, 1741, at Roxbury, Massachusetts. He was a brilliant scholar, and after his graduation from Harvard College studied medicine and became one of the best physicians in Boston. He early espoused the cause of liberty and became a firm supporter of the cause of the colonists. He possessed a fine, magnetic presence and an engaging address, and became known as a fluent writer and an eloquent speaker. In 1768 he was one of the influential members of the "Sons of Liberty," and it is recorded that "no important measures were taken without consulting him and his particular friends." He filled various high offices in the history of the colonies, and succeeded John Hancock as

President of the Provincial Congress. When the fourth anniversary of the Boston massacre arrived Warren solicited the privilege of delivering the anniversary address, in spite of the threats of the British officers that "They would take the life of any man who would dare speak on that occasion." In an eloquent speech, in which he pictured the wrongs of the colonists, he declared that "Resistance to tyrants is obedience to God."

Warren was a member of the Committee of Safety, and was commissioned a major-general four days previous to the battle of Bunker Hill. To a friend who urged him not to be present on that occasion, and who predicted his death if he participated in the inevitable engagement, Warren replied: "It is sweet to die for one's country." Warren reached the redoubt on Breed's Hill just before the battle opened, public business having prevented him from arriving sooner. Colonel Prescott offered him the command and asked for orders, but he replied that it was honor enough to serve under so brave an officer, and, borrowing a musket, rushed into the thickest of the fight. When the patriots' ammunition was spent, and the Americans had begun their sullen retreat, Warren was among the last to leave the field. A musket ball struck him in the head and killed him. He was buried on the spot where he fell, but during the next year his remains were removed to the family vault in Boston. Eventually they were placed in St. Paul's Church, in that city. In 1794 a monument was raised to his memory in Charlestown. In 1857 a statue of General Warren was enclosed in Bunker Hill Monument.

Congress met for the second time after the skirmish at Lexington and the more decisive engagement at Concord.

Joseph Warren. 21

A military Confederacy was formed, and General George Washington was the unanimous choice for commander-in-

Death of General Warren.

chief of the Continental Army. He declined compensation for his services, asking only that his expenses be defrayed. He immediately started for Boston, then occupied by a British army.   On his way there he was told that the patriots had stood their ground until their ammunition was expended, he exclaimed: " The liberties of our country are safe!"

GEORGE WASHINGTON.

GEORGE WASHINGTON, the first commander-in-chief of the armies of the United States, was born in Westmoreland County, Virginia, February 22, 1732. His father was Augustine Washington, whose ancestry can be traced back to the year 1183. The house in which Washington was born was burned down when he was a boy, but the spot where it stood is marked by a stone slab. When Washington was a boy of eleven years his father died, and he grew up under the tender care of his mother. His

education was that afforded by the common schools of the
neighborhood, but later he studied surveying and book-
keeping. His copy-books show that he wrote a very neat
hand. He excelled in athletic sports, and was proficient in
horsemanship. He was, from his youth, noted for honor
and truthfulness. Among the many anecdotes related of
the boyhood of Washington is the story of how he mutilated one of his father's cherry trees. When questioned
about the matter he did not deny it, but said:

" Father, I cannot tell a lie; I cut the tree."

" I had rather lose a thousand trees than find falsehood
in my son," replied his father, as he tenderly embraced
him.

Later in his life, at a social gathering given in honor of
her son, his venerable mother stood by his side, and, as
the clocks struck the hour of nine, she laid her hand upon
his shoulder, and said: " Come, George, it is time to retire. Late hours are injurious." Throughout his life Washington retained the habits of obedience, sobriety and punc-
tuality which he learned from his mother.

Washington's father left a large estate, and, after the
death of his brother Lawrence, Washington inherited the
estate of Mount Vernon. At the age of sixteen he began
the profession of a civil engineer, and spent a year in surveying the immense possessions of Lord Fairfax in the
Shenandoah Valley. Later he became the public surveyor,
and when nineteen was a major commanding a military district.

When England and France grappled in combat for the
possession of America, the Governor of Virginia sent the
young surveyor on a perilous mission across the trackless

Washington as a Young Man.

wilds to a French fort near Lake Erie. On his return he
was in great danger from the Indians, and nearly lost his
life in crossing the Allegheny River. For this service he
received the thanks of the Legislature of his State. As a
lieutenant-colonel he was sent, in 1754, with a regiment, to
build forts near the Ohio River, and to drive away the
French. He built Fort Necessity and killed or captured a
detachment of French soldiers. Later he was attacked by
a French force superior to his own and was obliged to surrender. Eventually he and his troops were allowed to
return to Virginia. He continued to serve during the remainder of the French and Indian war, and after the defeat of General Braddock he saved the army by his skill
and courage.

It was a beautiful summer's day when Braddock and his
army of two thousand men entered a defile upon the banks
of the Monongahela. The underbrush grew thick and high
and the great trees cast deep shadows on the army as it
confidently advanced with waving banners and gleaming
muskets. Suddenly a well-directed volley from the French,
who, with their Indian allies, had planned the ambuscade,
was poured into the British ranks. Not a foe was to be
seen, but their deadly rifles sent a message of death from
every tree and thicket. Nearly half of the British forces
fell under the murderous fire of the enemy, and then, un-
used to border warfare, they turned and fled in the utmost
confusion. General Braddock lost his life, but Washington, with cool valor, saved the British army from total destruction. He was in the most exposed and dangerous part
of the defile; two horses were shot under him and four bullets tore through his coat, but he seemed to bear a charmed

Washington at Fort Duquesne.   27

life. Rallying a few of the provincials, he placed them behind trees, and when the Indians rushed from their places of concealment to scalp the dead and tomahawk the dying, they were greeted with such a deadly fire that the shattered army was able to beat a hasty retreat.

Washington's health was now impaired by active warfare against the Indians, who were a constant menace to the settlements, and he retired from the service in 1759. In the same year he married Mrs. Martha Custis, a beautiful and wealthy young widow, and retired to his estate at Mount Vernon, leading the life of a rich planter, and becoming a member of the Virginia Legislature. He always took a deep interest in public affairs. When the odious " Stamp Act " was inflicted upon the colonists, Washington discountenanced " the use of all British merchandise taxed by Parliament to raise a revenue in America." Other oppressive measures followed, and when the first Continental Congress met in Philadelphia, Washington was a member of that immortal body, exhibiting the loftiest patriotism.

Washington was appointed Commander-in-Chief of the American Armies on June 15, 1775. He reached the camp before Boston on July 2, and immediately demonstrated his great organizing genius in making an army out of the raw material he found there. Everything was in confusion. Men were lodged in tents and huts; provisions and powder were scarce. His subordinates hampered him by divided counsels. Almost his first offensive movement was to fortify Dorchester Heights, a line of hills to the southwest of Boston. After a siege of eight months he compelled the British to leave Boston, and he then moved his army to New York. At this point he was attacked by a British army

The Declaration of Independence Read to the Army. 29

much larger than his own, commanded by Sir Henry Clinton. The battle of Long Island, near Brooklyn, was fought on August 27, 1776, and Washington was defeated. Obliged to give up New York to the enemy, he fought and lost the battle of White Plains, and then retreated through New Jersey, pursued by General Cornwallis. By heavy marching, Washington reached the Delaware River a few hours before Cornwallis, and, crowding his men into as few boats as possible, he began the perilous voyage to the Pennsylvania side. The battle with the storm that night was fiercer than a battle with the British would have been. Through snow and sleet and floating ice the half-starved, scantily-clad remnant of the Continental army fought their way and landed in Pennsylvania. On the Christmas morning following, he recrossed the river and fell upon the British army at Trenton, in the midst of their Christmas revelry, and took over a thousand prisoners. He recrossed the Delaware that night.

On the morning of January 3, 1777, Washington again crossed the Delaware and attacked the British at Princeton, compelling them to retreat. This battle was a decided victory for the Americans, but, owing to the condition of his army, scantily supplied with food, poorly clad, often barefooted, Washington was unable to follow up the victory as he wished, and so went into winter quarters. On September 11, Washington was defeated at the battle of Brandywine, and the British took Philadelphia. He was again defeated at Germantown, and afterwards wintered at Valley Forge, where the army suffered great privations. In June, 1778, the British retreated from Philadelphia, and the battle of Monmouth followed on June 28, with

Washington Crossing the Delaware.

the result that the British retreated after a hotly contested
engagement. Washington did not participate in any great
battles during 1779 and 1780, but in 1781 he besieged·

Cornwallis at Yorktown, Virginia. The British surrendered on October 19, 1781, and this act destroyed the last
hope of England's ever being able to subdue America. In

November, 1783, Great Britain acknowledged without reserve the independence of the United States.

Throughout the war
the labors of Washington
were incessant. He lost
more battles than he won,
but through his untiring
efforts, his self-sacrifice
and perseverance, he won

3　　Washington Inaugurated President.

the love and respect of all Americans, and when the colonies became free and independent he was acclaimed as the Father of his Country. For eight weary, toilsome, suffering years he held the command of the patriot forces, taking leave of the army on December 4, 1783, and retiring to private life. When the confederacy of states was formed into a nation, he was the unanimous choice for its first President, and wisely directed its affairs for two terms of four years each. In 1796 he sent a farewell address to Congress and refused another re-election. Again he retired to Mount Vernon, but when war with France was imminent he was called to be again Commander-in-Chief of the army. He died at Mount Vernon on December 14, 1799, before the French question was settled, after an illness of two days.

Washington's House, Mount Vernon.

Death of Washington.

ISRAEL PUTNAM.

ISRAEL PUTNAM, one of the best-known generals of the Revolution, was born in Salem, Massachusetts, January 7, 1718. He grew up a plain, sturdy farmer's boy, fond of athletic sports and excelling in all vigorous pastimes. A resolute courage was one of the most striking traits in his character, and it is related of him that he once administered a sound thrashing to a Boston boy who ridiculed him as a rustic. Putnam married early in life, and in 1840 became a farmer in the town of Pomfret, Connecticut, following this occupation for some fifteen years. It was during this period that he had his famous adventure with a wolf. It seems that this wolf committed depredations on the sheep in that neighborhood, and some of the farmers declared that it must be bewitched, for it had escaped them so many times. One morning, in winter, Putnam found two of his sheep killed, and a path in the snow which marked the way the wolf had gone. Getting his gun he followed the trail to a dark cave in the mountains. He explored the cave, and finding it deep he went for assistance, returning with a party of neighbors and a rope. Putnam tied the rope about his waist, and, with his gun in one hand and a torch in the other, was lowered into the darkness. Reaching solid ground he saw in a corner a pair of gleaming eyes and a row of glistening teeth. The beast rushed at him, but he did not flinch. He killed the

General Israel Putnam.

wolf with one shot, and was then drawn out of the cave by his friends.

When the French and Indian war broke out, Putnam was given a company of Connecticut troops. He was then thirty-six years of age, strong and fearless, delighting in a life of activity and danger. He was an invaluable ranger, or scout, and passed through many exciting adventures. At one time a fire broke out in Fort Edward, and the magazine was in danger. Putnam, who was stationed at no great distance from the fort, hurried to the scene. He sprang onto the roof of the burning building and poured water onto the flames as fast as it could be passed to him from the ground below. His mittens were burned from his hands, but a fresh pair was handed to him and he worked on until the structure fell in ruins. Then for more than an hour he continued to pour water onto the blazing mass, until the last spark was extinguished and the magazine, containing three hundred barrels of powder, was saved. Putnam's injuries were so severe that he was incapacitated for service for several weeks. After several hair-breadth escapes from the Indians, who had come to regard him as specially favored by their " Great Spirit," Putnam was captured by a band of Indians led by a French officer. He was tied to a tree and subjected to various tortures, and at last fagots of wood were piled around him and lighted. In a few moments he would have perished, but the French officer in command of the Indians rescued him. After a term of imprisonment an exchange of prisoners was affected and Putnam returned home. His next military service was in the war between England and Spain, in 1759, when he commanded a Connecticut regiment and assisted in the siege of Havana.

A Battle with the Indians.

After this war Putnam again retired to his farm and was plowing in the field when the news that patriot blood had been spilled at Lexington reached him. Without stopping to change his clothes, he mounted a horse and set off for the camp before Boston, leaving his plow in the field. The state of Connecticut made him a brigadier-general, and he threw himself into the patriot cause with all his resolution and courage. He participated in the battle of Bunker Hill, and after the evacuation of Boston by the British was placed in command of the city. Later he was in command of the American army at New York, and when that city was invested by the British he contrived to get his forces away in safety. Still later Washington placed him in command of Philadelphia and afterwards he operated in New Jersey, where his strategy and skill enabled him to successfully oppose large bodies of British troops.

In 1777, Putnam was defending Stamford. He had only one hundred and fifty militia-men and two old cannon. He was attacked by fifteen hundred British soldiers, but for a long time defended himself and kept the red-coats at bay. Finding, at last, that he must inevitably be overpowered by the force against him, he ordered his men to retreat into a neighboring swamp. He was the last man to leave the field, and being closely followed by British horsemen, he turned in the direction of "Breakneck Stairs," as they were called. These were one hundred steps cut in the solid rock in the hillside, and were used by the country people ascending the hill to go to church. Giving his horse the rein, he dashed down the steps at full speed. None of his pursuers dared follow him. Their shots flew about him, but he made the descent in safety, receiving no other injury than a bullet hole through his hat.

At another time, Putnam captured a Tory spy and sentenced him to be executed. Sir Henry Clinton, the British commander, sent a flag of truce to Putnam's camp, and claimed the man as a British soldier. Putnam's reply to the demand was: "Edmund Palmer, an officer in the enemy's service, was taken as a spy, lurking within our lines. He has been tried as a spy, condemned as a spy, and shall be executed as a spy, and the flag is ordered to depart immediately. P.S. He has been accordingly executed."

Putnam's military service continued until he was stricken with paralysis, in 1779. The old hero never recovered from this attack, but his death did not occur until May 19, 1790. He was buried with military honors, and remembered as a brave and noble man and a devoted patriot.

NATHAN HALE.

NATHAN HALE, the young martyr, patriot and hero, was born in Coventry, Connecticut, June 6, 1755. His father was Richard Hale, a descendant of one Robert Hale, who settled in Massachusetts in 1632. As an infant, Nathan was feeble, but as he advanced in years he developed into a robust child; sweet tempered and possessed of many graces of person. He loved out-of-door sports and excelled in all athletic games. He was brought up strictly, being taught to observe the Christian Sabbath and to reverence ministers and magistrates. His parents destined him for the ministry, and when but sixteen years of age he entered Yale College. He graduated from this institution in 1773 with the highest honors. His personal appearance is described as being notable.

"He was almost six feet in height, perfectly proportioned, and in figure and deportment he was the most manly man I ever met," is the testimony of one who knew him well. His chest was broad; his muscles were firm; his face wore a most benign expression; his complexion was roseate; his eyes were light blue and beamed with intelligence; his hair was soft and light brown in color; and his speech was rather low, sweet, and musical. His personal beauty and grace of manner were most charming.

After graduating from college, Hale became a school teacher at East Haddam, Connecticut, and then became an

instructor in a
high-grade gram-
mar school at
New London, in
the same state.
Here he made
many loving
friends, and
moved in the best
society. He was
betrothed to a
beautiful girl
named Alice
Adams, who was
one of his pupils.
His orderly life
was interrupted
by the news of
bloodshed at Lex-
ington and Con-
cord, and he em-
braced the patriot
cause at once.
"Let us march
immediately and
never lay down
our arms until we
have obtained
our independ-
ence!" were his
words to those
who assembled at
the hastily called
town meeting.

Volunteers were enrolled that night and Hale was among them. The next day he bade farewell to his pupils and started for the patriot camp before Boston. Later Hale became a lieutenant, and participated in the siege of Boston. He was then made a captain and accompanied the American army to New York. While there he performed a hazardous feat. With a boat's crew, he surprised a British supply vessel, drove the crew below decks and brought the prize to the city, where her cargo was distributed among the hungry soldiers of the army.

After the Americans were defeated at Long Island, Washington was informed that the British intended to make an advance up the river. It was important to decide whether the city of New York should be defended or abandoned. It became necessary to send a competent person, in disguise, into the British lines to learn the intentions of the enemy. A number of officers were called together, the hazardous nature of the undertaking was explained, and a volunteer was called for. While the conference was going on, Hale entered, bearing the marks of recent illness, and exclaimed, " I will undertake it!" His friends endeavored to dissuade him, but he was not to be turned from his purpose. He knew that if he was caught his death would be that of a spy, yet he said: " I wish to be useful; and every kind of service necessary for the public good becomes honorable by being necessary. If the exigencies of my country demand a peculiar service, its claims to the performance of that service are imperious."

Washington personally gave him his instructions and he set out on his perilous mission. In the dress of a citizen. and by representing himself as a "schoolmaster and a loyalist disgusted with the rebel cause," he visited the British camp. made plans of the fortifications, and obtained the information he sought for. On his way back, he was arrested while looking for his friends, who were to meet him with a boat. He was taken on board a British ship, where he was stripped and searched. The plans of the fortifications were found in his shoes, where he had secreted them, and then he was taken to General Howe's headquarters and confined in a greenhouse belonging to the mansion. This was on Saturday night, September 21. Hale accepted his fate like a man and a true patriot. He frankly told his rank and the purpose for which he entered the British lines. Early on the following day he was turned over to William Cunningham, the provost-marshal of New York, who treated him with the greatest barbarity and heaped insults upon him. His last hours were made as miserable as the harshness of his jailor could make them. He asked for a chaplain and then for a Bible. Both requests were denied. He wrote letters to friends and relatives, and to his betrothed, but instead of sending them, Cunningham first read them and then tore them up before the eyes of the young hero. When the sun rose, Hale was led from his prison and executed.

An excellent statue has been erected in New York city, on the spot where the martyred patriot stood for the last time. His arms are bound behind his back; but with throat bare and head erect, he seems almost repeating again his last words:—" I regret that I have only one life to give to my country!"

ETHAN ALLEN.

ETHAN ALLEN, one of the best known figures in the war of the Revolution, was born on January 10, 1737, in Litchfield, Connecticut. Very little is known of his early life, except that he was one of a large family of children and grew up to be a sturdy, independent man and an earnest advocate of liberty. In 1772, we hear of him residing in Bennington, Vermont, a trusted leader of the " Green Mountain Boys," as the bold mountaineers of that state were termed at that time. He also represented them in presenting their claims to certain land grants to which they laid claim. These cases were decided at Albany, and were against Allen's clients, who immediately determined to hold their lands by force. Soon they were in constant warfare with the royal officers who came to evict them, and several of these sheriffs were whipped by the settlers. The Green Mountain Boys banded together to resist the injustice of the crown, and in Allen they found a determined and resourceful leader. Finally a price was put upon his head by Governor Tryon, but Allen continued in what he considered was his line of duty, acting only on the defensive, however. Matters were in this condition when news of the massacre at Lexington reached these hardy men, and abandoning their private wrongs, they set out to play their part in the contest for liberty.

Soon a plan for the capture of Fort Ticonderoga was on foot, as this was a point of great strategic importance.

Ethan Allen.

47

Men from Connecticut and Massachusetts met at Bennington, and joined Colonel Allen and his Green Mountain Boys. Allen was appointed commander of the expedition, which comprised some two hundred and thirty men. On the morning of May 10, 1775, eighty-three men had been taken across the lake and landed near the fort. Great difficulty had been experienced in procuring boats, and as day was breaking, Allen did not dare to wait for more men to cross before making the attack. He addressed his men and told them of the hazardous nature of the undertaking, but every one of them volunteered to attack at once. A sentry snapped his piece at Allen and then fled into the fort, whence the Americans followed him. Another sentry made a pass at one of Allen's officers, but Allen wounded him, and he cried for quarter. Then Allen compelled him to tell where the commander of the fort, Captain De la Place, slept, and when he reached the-room, which was in the second story, he called loudly to that officer to come forth instantly or he would sacrifice the entire garrison. Soon Captain De la Place appeared only partially dressed. Allen ordered him to deliver the fort instantly. The captain asked by what authority he demanded it and Allen replied: " In the name of the Great Jehovah and the Continental Congress." De la Place tried to parley, but Allen waved his sword over his head and again demanded the surrender of the garrison. The British commander complied and ordered his men to be paraded without arms, and so the famous Fort Ticonderoga fell into the hands of the brave Green Mountain Boys.

A few days later, Crown Point was captured by Seth Warner, who was sent there by Allen for that purpose.

Benedict Arnold, who was then an earnest and patriotic American, was to have had command of the expedition against Ticonderoga, but the Green Mountain Boys would have no leader but Allen. Arnold submitted gracefully and went as a volunteer, marching side by side with Allen,

Montreal.

and entering the fort with him. After receiving pay for his men, and also permission to raise a new regiment, Allen joined General Schuyler as a volunteer, and was sent by that officer on a mission to Canada. He returned, and was raising a force of men to operate with General Montgomery, when he was induced to join a Major Brown

4

in an attack upon Montreal. Brown failed to appear at
the appointed time and place, and Allen and his handful of
men were captured and taken before Colonel Prescott,
who inquired if he was the man who took Ticonderoga.
Allen replied that he was. Prescott broke into a terrible
rage and ordered him bound hand and foot on the Gaspee.
To Allen's complaints of the brutality of this treatment
Prescott turned a deaf ear. At last Allen was taken to
England, and so many people went to see the hero of
Ticonderoga that he became quite a distinguished prisoner. Allen was exchanged for a Lieutenant-Colonel
Campbell, and his captivity of two and a half years was
over.

After reporting to General Washington, at Valley Forge,
Allen returned to his Green Mountain home, where he
was enthusiastically received. Congress voted him the
pay of a lieutenant-colonel for the time of his imprisonment, and made him a brevet-colonel in the Continental
army. Allen now renewed his efforts in behalf of the independence of Vermont, and was made a general of militia
by the people of that state. When the independence of
Vermont became a fact, General Allen became a member
of the state Assembly.

Many anecdotes illustrating the strong points of Allen's
nature have been related. The following is one of them:

, " On one occasion, an individual to whom he was indebted commenced a suit against him. Allen, being unable to pay the debt, employed a lawyer to have the execution of legal processes against him postponed for a short
period. As an easy measure to effect this and throw the
case over to the next session of the court, the lawyer

denied the genuineness of the signature. Allen, who was present, stepped angrily forward, and exclaimed to his astonished counsel: 'Sir, I did not employ you to come here and lie! I wish you to tell the truth. The note is a good one—the signature is mine; all I want is for the court to grant me sufficient time to make the payment.' It is needless to add that the plaintiff acceded to his wishes."

After the capture of Ticonderoga, the pastor of a church in Bennington—a Rev. Mr. Dewey—preached a sermon on Allen's exploit, and in his prayer thanked the Lord for the victory. Allen was present at the service and was much pleased, but as the preacher continued his thanksgiving, he called out:

" Parson Dewey!"

The preacher prayed on, not heeding the interruption.

Allen exclaimed still louder:

" Parson Dewey!"

No response. At last Allen was exasperated, and sprang to his feet, while he fairly roared out, for the third time:

" Parson Dewey!"

At last the praying clergyman opened his eyes and gazed in astonishment at Allen. Allen then said, with energy:

" Parson Dewey! please make mention of my being there."

Vermont owes a great debt to Ethan Allen, and she has reared a statue in his memory, which stands in the State House at Montpelier. The old hero died on his farm, near Colchester, Vermont, on February 13, 1789.

JOHN STARK.

JOHN STARK, an incorruptible patriot, was born on August 28, 1728, at Londonderry, New Hampshire. His family was of Scotch extraction. When eight years of age the Stark family moved to Manchester, and for nearly twenty years young Stark led the life of a New England settler, varying farming with trapping and hunting. He was fond of adventure and possessed of an athletic frame capable of great endurance. It was during this period of his life that he set off on a hunting expedition, accompanied by his brother and two friends. The young men separated temporarily and John Stark was suddenly surrounded and seized by Indians. The Indians, knowing that he had companions, asked Stark where they were. He gave the wrong direction, and for a time the savages were baffled, but they afterwards came upon the remainder of the party. One they quickly made a prisoner and then ordered Stark to hail the others, who were in a boat, and order them to come ashore. Instead, Stark warned them of their danger, and when the Indians fired upon them he struck up their guns and diverted their aim. Twice he did this, but one of the young men was killed. Stark then called to the one who was left to fly for his life, and he did so and escaped. This was Stark's brother. Enraged by their failure to capture the entire party, the Indians fell on Stark and beat him terribly.

John Stark.

At the Indian camp Stark and his friend were compelled to run the gauntlet. During this ordeal Eastman barely escaped with his life; but Stark did better, for he snatched a club from one of his tormentors and cleared a path for himself as he ran. This raised him in the estimation of his captors, and later, when he threw his hoe into the river and refused to work for them, they adopted him into their tribe. He was eventually ransomed, as was his companion, but the price put upon each showed that the Indians held them at a different valuation, as they required one hundred and three dollars for Stark, while for Eastman they accepted sixty dollars.

Stark's first military service was in the French and Indian war. He served in a corps of Rangers as a lieutenant. Stark was one of an expedition under Major Rogers, fitted out to operate around Lake Champlain. Their march was partly on the ice of the lake and partly through the snow on the shore. They were suddenly attacked, and the enemy made terrible havoc in their ranks. Stark held them at bay until that portion of the band immediately under Rogers rallied. Then the little band of Americans fought on through the winter's afternoon. Stark was wounded in the wrist, and a bullet shattered the lock of his gun. He wrenched another weapon from the grasp of a dying Frenchman, and fought on until the enemy withdrew as darkness came on. All night the weary line of Americans dragged through the woods, and when the wounded could go no further Stark, with two companions, marched forty miles to get aid, accomplishing the feat on snow shoes. Without waiting for rest, he at once turned back and covered the ground again. Reaching his com-

The Indians Ambush Stark's Command.

rades, he placed the wounded on sleds and started with them for Fort William Henry, the point of safety, thus covering one hundred and twenty miles on snow shoes, in the dead of winter, in less than forty hours, and this after fighting a superior force for hours. For this feat of endurance, and for the humanity displayed in it, Stark was made a captain.

After some service under Lord Howe, Stark returned home and married. Shortly afterwards he was employed in road making, and then again retired to private life, where he remained until the echoes of Concord and Lexington startled him from his peaceful occupations. Then he entered heart and soul into the patriot cause, and became colonel of a regiment. He was stationed at Medford, but joined the patriots at Bunker Hill during the hottest of the fight, leading his sturdy New Hampshire boys across Charlestown neck through a merciless British fire. Behind the historic rail-fence filled with hay, these brave men fought with the steadiness of veterans, and were among the last to leave the field.

A characteristic anecdote is told of Stark upon his return to Medford after the battle of Bunker Hill. It seems that the paymaster there did not like Stark and refused to pay the men, alleging that the pay-rolls were not correct. He did this on three occasions, and then the men appealed to their leader. Stark said: " The regiment has made him three visits; he shall now make them one in return." A guard was sent and it brought the paymaster into camp, the drums and fifes playing the " Rogue's March."

Late in 1776, Stark and his men were sent to reinforce

Washington, and before the battle of Trenton the blunt old soldier told Washington:

" You have depended a long time on spades and pick-axes, but if you wish ever to establish the independence of the country, you must rely on firearms."

Washington replied:

" To-morrow we march on Trenton, and I have appointed you to command the advance guard of the right wing."

After the battle of Princeton, in which he participated, Stark went to New Hampshire and recruited his regiment. Being justly incensed at the promotion of junior officers, while he was left out of the list, he retired from the army, declaring that an officer who would tamely submit to such an indignity was not fit to be trusted. He lost none of his patriotism, however, and later accepted the command of state troops, refusing to fight under the orders of Congress. Men flocked from all directions to fight under his leadership, and he was ordered to place his command under general orders; but he stubbornly refused to do this, and in August, 1777, marched to encounter the enemy, who was marching through Vermont. On August 16, he fought and won the famous battle of Bennington. The British were intrenched upon a line, and when Stark saw them he turned to his troops with the now historic remark:

" See there, men! there are the red-coats. Before night they are ours, or Molly Stark's a widow."

The battle began with a terrible fire of musketry, but the militia fought with the precision of veterans, routed the British horse and foot soldiers, streamed over the breastworks and won the gallant field.

Stark continued in the militia service for some time. Then Congress gave him a vote of thanks for the victory at Bennington and a commission as brigadier-general. He served through the war and then retired to his farm. He lived to the ripe age of ninety-four years, and was buried with military honors.

NATHANIEL GREENE.

NATHANIEL GREENE was born in Warwick, Rhode Island, on May 27, 1742. His father was a Quaker preacher, and his son was early instructed in the tenets of that sect. When old enough to assist in the labors of the farm, the boy was put to work, clad in the sober garb affected by the Quakers. After a time he was taken from farm work and placed at a forge owned by his father. But whether in the fields or at the anvil, Greene expended a good deal of his youthful energy in athletic sports and became very fond of dancing. In order to indulge in this pastime, he would steal out of the house after the family were asleep; but on one occasion he returned from a ball at an early hour in the morning to find his father waiting for him with a horsewhip. He had just time to slip some shingles under his coat from a convenient pile, and in the subsequent chastisement found the punishment much mitigated for his resort to this novel armor.

Books soon claimed the attention of the young Quaker,

Nathaniel Greene.

and while engaged at his labors he found time to master
the difficult problems of Euclid without assistance; to
read Horace and Cæsar, and even Blackstone. At twenty
years of age he was able to take part in the political dis-
cussions of the day. When war clouds gathered about the
colonies he threw away his Quaker prejudices and studied
military science. For this, the people in whose faith he
was born took him to account, but he remained firm to
his convictions and joined an independent military company. He was a member of the General Assembly of
Rhode Island in 1770. Four years later he married.

After Lexington, Greene started for Boston, and was
soon made a major-general of Rhode Island troops. These
he put into good condition, and after the battle of Bunker
Hill joined Washington at Cambridge. Washington sent
him to occupy Long Island, but falling sick, Putnam was
given charge of the operations there. Greene participated
in the battle of Harlem Heights, and was with Washington in his retreat through New Jersey. He commanded a
division at the battle of Trenton, and also at Princeton,
exhibiting in both engagements perfect coolness and resolution. At Brandywine, Greene was at the rear of the
American army, but feeling that his men were needed at
the front, he marched them four miles in forty-nine minutes, and arrived in time to check the scattering fugitives and make a bold stand with his own men.

General Greene commanded a division of the American
army at the Battle of Germantown. His aide-de-camp.
Major Burnet, wore his hair in a queue in the old-fashioned
style. While the battle was at its height the Major's queue
was shot away by a musket ball. "Don't be in a hurry,

Major," said Greene; "just dismount and get that long queue." It was but a few minutes later that another shot from the enemy cut away a large powdered curl from Gen-

Battle of Cowpens.

eral Greene's forehead. The British were in hot pursuit of the Americans at this moment, but Major Burnet said: "Don't be in a hurry, General; just dismount and get that

long curl." The advice was not taken, however. Greene
performed splendid services at Germantown, and then
with the troops went into winter quarters at Valley Forge,
where he was made Quartermaster-General, and did much
to reorganize the army.

Greene served at Monmouth with his usual gallantry
and was then sent to Rhode Island to coöperate with Lafayette and Sullivan. From Rhode Island, Greene was sent
to New Jersey and heroically defended Springfield in that
state. He presided at the court-martial which tried and
condemned the unfortunate Major André, and later was
in command at West Point. From that position he was
sent south to retrieve, if possible, the reverses of the
patriot cause in that section. He found an army without
money, without stores, destitute of clothing, of arms, of
everything necessary for an effective force. Of two thousand men barely eight hundred were fit for service; but
his officers were the bravest of the brave and patriots to
the core. Greene employed every possible moment in
drilling his troops, and to gain time for this sent out de-
tachments to annoy and harrass the enemy without bringing on a general engagement. He led Cornwallis a terrible
chase, and then came the battle of Cowpens, where Washington cut Tarleton's crack dragoons to pieces, and Morgan's militia drove the British infantry before them, like
veterans. Morgan was obliged to retreat after the battle was
gained, for he could not cope with Cornwallis's army, which
was close upon him. That general strained every nerve to
cut him off, but failing in this endeavored to prevent his
junction with Greene. In this he also failed, and then
Greene took up his memorable and masterly retreat

through the Carolinas, in which he out-generaled the British commander. Through rain and mud, Greene fled for twenty days, covering two hundred and fifty miles. He crossed three large rivers, and baffled his adversary at every point, finally bringing his army to a place of safety and covering his own name with renown.

At Guilford Court House, Greene gave battle to Cornwallis, but was eventually compelled to retreat after inflicting a terrible loss on the enemy. As soon as Cornwallis could collect his wounded, he, too, fearing that his victory would be dearly bought if he remained on the field, fled rapidly from the scene of the engagement, having suffered a loss of six hundred killed and wounded. Greene sent a detachment of cavalry to hang on the rear of the British army, and himself pursued them towards Wilmington. But at length his army began to murmur at the hardships they were compelled to undergo. The term of enlistment of many had expired; Greene could not supply them with provisions. and so, after thanking them for their bravery, he saw them depart for their own homes.

With an army reduced to one-third of its size, Greene now led it into South Carolina and fought the battle of Hobkirk's Hill, which he lost through no fault of his own, and then moved on to the post known as Ninety-six. He made a noble assault on the position, but was unable to carry it. The British evacuated it, however, shortly afterwards. Through all these reverses Greene's spirit was undaunted. He fought the enemy and harrassed it continually. After an engagement he would rest his troops and then put them in motion again. In his own words: "We will seek the enemy wherever we can find them, unless they take refuge within the gates of Charleston." He shared the hardships of his men, and on the night before the battle of Eutaw Springs, as on many other occasions, he slept on the ground in the midst of his soldiers.

Greene won the battle of Eutaw Springs, but he suffered severe losses. Both armies buried their dead under a flag of truce, and then the sickly season set in, and he moved his army to the Santee hills. After the surrender of Cornwallis, Greene boldly took the field again, and finally drove the British into Charleston. Closer and closer he drew his lines about the city, and in spite of the terrible condition of his own army, who were dying by scores in the scorching sun, destitute of clothing and provisions, he held on until the British evacuated the city. Then Greene entered and received an ovation from the multitudes who knew the privations that he and his army had passed through.

After the peace General Greene made his home at Mulberry Grove, Georgia, where he died on June 19, 1786.

ANTHONY WAYNE.

ANTHONY WAYNE, a brilliant officer of the Revolution, and afterwards commander-in-chief of the armies of the United States, was born in Chester County, Pennsylvania, January 1, 1745. His early education was at the hands of a relative, and afterwards at the Philadelphia Academy, where he appears to have distinguished himself in mathematics. It is also said of him that he had a liking for military studies as well. Leaving school at seventeen years of age, he became a farmer and land-surveyor, and was married five years later.

When the colonies grew restive under the oppressive measures of Great Britain, Wayne openly declared that hostilities would follow, and immediately began to raise volunteers for the war which he deemed inevitable. Congress made him a colonel when his prediction became true, and his first service was in Canada. He was wounded at Three Rivers, and then commanded at Fort Ticonderoga, joining Washington in New Jersey in 1777. He was now a brigadier-general, and had been complimented for distinguished bravery and skill.

Wayne bore a conspicuous part at Brandywine, and at Germantown his horse was shot under him. In this last battle he covered the retreat of the Americans. Subsequently, at Valley Forge, Wayne commanded a foraging expedition and brought much relief to the destitute army in the shape of cattle and provisions of various kinds. At

5

Monmouth, Wayne distinguished himself by his bravery,
and was commended by Washington in his official letter
to Congress.

The storming of Stony Point, on the Hudson River,
was assigned to General Wayne, and he successfully carried the position by assault, shortly after midnight of July
15, 1779. Its natural defenses had been strengthened, and,
with its strong garrison, was regarded as almost impregna-
ble. Wayne divided his forces into two columns, and each
man at the same time was ordered " to fix a piece of white
paper in the most conspicuous part of his hat or cap to
distinguish him from the enemy," and a watchword, " The
fort's our own," was communicated to each, with orders
to give it " with repeated and loud voice when the works
were forced, and not before." Scaling the parapet, and
creeping through the embrasures on either side, the assail-
ants raised the cry agreed upon, and drove the garrison before them, notwithstanding the most desperate resistance
was offered. While this terrible hand-to-hand contest was
raging within the fort, Wayne, who had been wounded in
the head by a musket ball, was lying near the spot where
he fell; but when the enemy had surrendered, as it soon
did, he was carried into the fort, " bleeding, but in triumph." Three hearty cheers from his victorious troops
formed the salute under which the daring general was carried into the fort to receive the submission of the garrison, and again " The fort's our own!" broke out in the in-
spiration of the moment.

In 1781, Wayne was with Lafayette in Virginia. Lafayette ordered him to attack the rear guard of Cornwallis's
army, thinking the main body had passed over a river.

Anthony Wayne.   67

Wayne fell upon the British as directed, but found it to
be the army itself. Grasping the situation, he made such
a vigorous charge that Cornwallis thought the entire
American army was upon him and began to prepare for a
general engagement. Under cover of his movements
Wayne was able to withdraw his troops, thus extricating
them from a perilous position.

After the surrender of Yorktown, Wayne joined General
Greene and operated in Georgia, where the British outnumbered him three to one. But his indomitable spirit
rose above every obstacle, and he drove the enemy from
one point to another until he virtually wrested the state
from the British. In speaking of this campaign, Wayne
said:

" The duty we have done in Georgia was more difficult
than that imposed upon the children of Israel; they had
only to make bricks without straw, but we have had pro-
vision, forage, and almost every other apparatus of war to
procure without money; boats, bridges, etc., to build without materials, except those taken from the stump; and
what was more difficult than all—to make Whigs out of
Tories. But this we have effected, and have wrested the
country out of the hands of the enemy, with the exception
only of the town of Savannah."

Two tribes of Indians—the Choctaws and the Creeks—
had been induced to join the British forces. Wayne fell
upon and completely routed the former and then turned
his attention to the Creeks. He instructed his men to
rely entirely upon the bayonet and the sword, and led
them to a defile through which the enemy must pass.
Wayne and his men reached the pass at the same time

"The Fort's Our Own!"

that the enemy entered it, and although outnumbered he
fell upon them with such impetuosity that they fled before
him. Later, the Creeks crept stealthily up to Wayne's
camp and with a terrible war-whoop drove in his pickets.
For a few moments all was terror and confusion, but
Wayne rallied his men and led them against their foes.
With his own hand he cut down a tall chief, who, in his
death throes, fired at him, but missed his aim and killed
Wayne's horse. The conflict was a short one, and soon the
savages fled in dismay. Shortly afterwards the British
evacuated Savannah and peace soon followed.

Wayne was not allowed to rest in peace, however. An
Indian war followed that of the Revolution, and Wayne
was made commander-in-chief of the army. He conducted operations so well that a long peace with the red
men was effected. Wayne's death came while exercising
the functions of an Indian Commissioner in what was then
called the Northwest. He died on December 14, 1796,
at Presque Isle, and was buried there, but later his remains
were removed to his native county and a monument was
erected to his memory.

Wayne was one of the most popular men in the army,
and was known the country over as " Mad Anthony." It
is said that " this name was originally given by a witless
fellow in the camp, who used always to take a circuit
when he came near Wayne, and, shaking his head, mutter
to himself, ' Mad Anthony! mad Anthony!' It was so
characteristic of Wayne, however, that the troops universally adopted it."

FRANCIS MARION.

THERE is perhaps more of romance in the career of Francis Marion; more of personal adventure and daring than in that of any other general of the Revolution. He was born in 1732, at Winyah, South Carolina. His ancestors were French Huguenots, and from them he inherited a disposition that enabled him to serve his country well in the hour of its need.

Marion was a feeble, sickly child until he was about twelve years of age. Then he began to take an interest in athletic pursuits, and soon acquired a frame capable of enduring the hardships of a settler's life. When fifteen years of age he went to sea, but was shipwrecked. He was rescued, however, and, thoroughly cured of a sea life, returned to his father's farm. His first military service was against the Indians. At one time he led thirty men against a band of Cherokees, losing twenty-one in the skirmish that ensued.

When the Revolutionary War broke out Marion was a member of the Provincial Congress of South Carolina, and is described as being small in stature, with a swarthy, thoughtful face, and piercing black eyes. He immediately began to recruit men for the patriot cause, and being thoroughly acquainted with military tactics soon had his men thoroughly drilled and disciplined. There was a magnetism about the man that few could resist, and it was esteemed an honor to serve under his leadership. When the

British attacked Fort Moultrie, Marion and his men were
part of the brave garrison, and the last shot from the fort
is credited to Marion's own hand. After the British ships
withdrew Marion remained in command of the fort.

After the fall of Charleston, and with the British in
possession of the surrounding country, Marion, after being hunted from one place of concealment to another, with
a handful of men joined General Gates. They were a sorry
looking lot—their garments tattered and nondescript,
their arms rusty, the horses presenting much the same appearance as their riders. In 1780, Marion became the
leader of a band of patriots, undisciplined, but brave, and
also skilled in the use of firearms. He was commissioned
a general by the Governor of South Carolina, and soon the
little band of some thirty men was increased and became
known as Marion's Brigade. Marion and his men then entered upon a career of toil and privation, but they became
well disciplined and performed such daring deeds that
they were feared alike by the British and the Tories. It
became the highest honor to which a man could aspire to
belong to Marion's band. Every man was a dead shot and
a dashing rider, skilled in the use of the sabre. Marion led
them to hiding places in the swamps and then emerged
and struck heavy blows upon the enemy. His troop became a terror and a menace to the Tories in particular,
but no plans to capture the "Swamp Fox," as they called
him, were ever successful.

Well-planned attempts on the part of the enemy to
crush Marion utterly failed. He would make a descent
upon a British camp or a Tory gathering, and then enter
the swamps and lie concealed where his enemies did not

Francis Marion.

dare to follow him. The fare of these brave men was of the rudest description. They had no money, and subsisted as best they could. Marion's principal camp was at Snow's Island, and there the hardy men who followed his fortunes rested in picturesque array when not engaged in active duty. The place was easily defended, and trusty rifles guarded every avenue of approach. There is a story of a young British officer who visited this camp to arrange for an exchange of prisoners. He was led to the camp blind-folded, and when the bandage was removed from his eyes he looked bewildered upon the scene. He saw the par-tisan soldiers resting beneath the tall pines, their horses tethered close by; he saw their leader, slight of stature, with none of the externals of a successful general, and could hardly believe that this was the hardy band whose very name filled the hearts of their enemies with terror. The business that brought him completed, dinner was served—sweet potatoes baked in the ashes and served upon pieces of bark.

"Doubtless this is an accidental meal," said the officer; "you live better in general?"

"No," was the reply; "we often fare much worse."

"Then I hope at least you draw noble pay to compen-sate?"

"Not a cent, sir," replied Marion; "not a cent."

In telling this incident, upon his return to the British camp, the officer said: "What chance have we against such men?" It is related that he resigned his commission, and did not serve again throughout the war.

It has been said of Marion that his only drink was vine-gar and water, mixed, and that:—

"His favorite time for marching was with the setting
sun, and then it was known that the march would con-
tinue all night. Before striking any sudden blow he has
been known to march sixty or seventy miles, taking no

One of Marion's Men

other food in twenty-four hours than a meal of cold potatoes and a draught of cold water. His scouts were out in
all directions and at all hours. They were taught a peculiar and shrill whistle, which at night would be heard at

a most astonishing distance. They did the double duty of patrols and spies. They hovered about the posts of the enemy, crouching in the thickets or darting along the plain, picking up prisoners and information and spoils together."

Marion successfully evaded every expedition sent to capture him, but one British band penetrated his camp on Snow Island and destroyed it. This greatly disheartened Marion, but his men followed his fortunes, even when they seemed to be at the lowest ebb. He now set out in pursuit of Colonel Watson, a British officer who had been very active in dogging his footsteps, but Watson fled, and Marion, joining his forces to those of "Light Horse" Harry, invested Fort Watson. As neither party had cannon, Marion resorted to an expedient which proved successful. He ordered trees cut down and made into logs and these he piled up during the night, so that when daylight dawned he was able to send a shower of bullets into the garrison, which soon surrendered. Later, Marion joined General Greene and continued to render invaluable services to the country. He was constantly engaged in harassing the enemy. After Greene drove the enemy into Charleston, Marion resumed his duties as a legislator, turning over his brigade to Captain Horry, a trusted officer of his; but, learning that the British were bent upon dispersing it in his absence, he took the field again and saved it.

After the war Marion continued active in his legislative duties, and married a lady of about his own age. He died at the age of sixty-three, a pure and lofty patriot, holding country and liberty dearer than all things else in life.

HUGH MERCER.

HUGH MERCER, a brigadier-general in the war of the Revolution, was a Scotchman who emigrated to America and made his home on the western frontier of Pennsylvania. We first hear of him in Provincial affairs as a captain in the Indian wars of 1755. Of his earlier life we know very little, but he was in the army of Prince Charles Edward, and participated in the battle of Culloden. By profession he was a physician. He was so badly wounded at Braddock's defeat that he was unable to keep up with the demoralized British troops. Hidden behind a log he watched the savages scalping the dead and dispatching the wounded. He dragged himself to a stream of water, of which he drank, and then kept on the track of the retreating army as rapidly as his shattered shoulder would allow. When nearly exhausted by famine and the pain of his wound he succeeded in killing a rattlesnake. Skinning it with one hand, he devoured a portion of it raw, and so, feeding on the reptile from time to time, he managed to reach Fort Cumberland, more dead than alive.

Mercer at one time commanded Fort Duquesne, and there made the acquaintance of Washington, who was then a young officer in the Provincial service. Later, when the colonists asserted their rights, and were fighting for their independence, Mercer joined the patriot army and was made a brigadier-general. His early services for his adopted country were with Washington at New York, and the commander-in-chief found him in every way worthy of his confidence. He accompanied Washington on the dreary retreat throughout New Jersey, when a deep cloud of gloom hovered over the entire country; but his belief that liberty would triumph remained unshaken. He was among the first to advocate an aggressive campaign against the British in New Jersey, and became one of Washington's most valued advisers.

When the battle of Princeton was fought Mercer led one of the attacking columns, and, throwing himself between the main body of the British troops and their reserves, brought about the action. A rapid march of eighteen miles brought Washington's army to the eastern skirts of Princeton on the morning of January 3, 1777. The contending armies being about equal in forces and artillery, the ground was fiercely contested. The patriots were at first thrown into some confusion by the vigorous resistance they encountered, but by great personal exertions, in which his own life was recklessly exposed, Washington rallied his men, and leading his raw troops to within thirty yards of the enemy, made a headlong charge. The British regiments broke and fled, unable to resist the terrible onslaught of such men.

Mercer fought bravely, and when his horse was shot under him, continued to fight on foot against terrible odds. He was wounded, and when taken prisoner asked for honorable treatment. Instead, the brutal British soldiers felled him to the earth and then plunged their bayonets into his body. Thinking him dead, they left him where he lay, but he was found and carried to a neighboring

GEN. HUGH MERCER.

farmhouse, bleeding from thirteen wounds. He lingered in agony for a few days, and then died, a martyr in the cause of liberty, with a prayer for his family and his country upon his lips.

Battle of Princeton. Death of Mercer.

RICHARD MONTGOMERY.

RICHARD MONTGOMERY was born in Ireland, December 2, 1736, but emigrated to this country in 1772. At the age of eighteen years he was holding a commission in the British army, and later distinguished himself at the siege of Louisburg, earning a lieutenantcy for his gallantry. Still later he served under Amherst; was present at the sieges of Montreal and Quebec, and was made a captain for distinguished services against the French in the West Indies. Upon his arrival in America he settled near New York and married. It was not until after the battle of Bunker Hill that Montgomery really threw in his fortunes with the country of his adoption, although he had been a member of the first provincial convention of New York.

When Congress voted in favor of the invasion of Canada, Montgomery, who had been made a brigadier-general, began his military service for the colonies under General Schuyler. He was a man of great courage, and when Schuyler was prostrated by sickness, Montgomery took command of the expedition. He quelled a serious mutiny among his troops, and then, being short of ammunition, attacked Fort Chambly and took it, obtaining a much needed supply in this way. Other successes followed, including the capture of Montreal.

Arnold was then investing Quebec, but was in bad straits.

6

Montgomery marched to his relief, making a toilsome march over frozen ground and through drifting snows. His troops encountered great hardships on the way, but Montgomery shared their privations and eventually brought

Quebec.

his undisciplined command to the walls of Quebec. The combined forces of Arnold and Montgomery could do little more than harrass the besieged. Their few cannon could make no impression on the walls of the city and their operations were hampered by the ice and snow. The troops

General Richard Montgomery.

were miserably clad for any climate, and in the rigors of a
Canadian winter it was with difficulty that they could
move their benumbed limbs, or serve the cannon, which
were mounted upon blocks of ice. Small-pox broke out
in the camp, and the army was on the verge of mutiny.
With these conditions staring him in the face, Montgomery,
who was in command of the combined forces, called a
council of war at which it was decided to make an assault
upon the fortifications.

Before daylight on the last day of December, 1775, two
officers were sent to make a feint against the upper town,
while Montgomery and Arnold should storm the defenses
of the lower town. The patriots set out in the dark and
gloom of the winter morning, Montgomery at the head
of one column, while Arnold led the other—the forlorn
hope.   Success was with Montgomery at first, but huge
masses of ice impeded the progress of his soldiers and gave
the British time to recover from the panic into which they
were thrown when the Americans surprised the first battery. Struggling on through snow and ice, another battery confronted the handful of brave souls. For an instant
they seemed to hesitate. Waving his sword over his head,
Montgomery shouted: "Men of New York! You will not
fear to follow where your general leads—forward!"

Montgomery fell at the first discharge from the British
cannon, and seeing their leader stretched upon the snow,
the troops recoiled and fled.

Arnold intrepidly led his men against another battery,
receiving a musket-ball in the leg, and Captain Morgan assumed command. Under his leadership, the battery was
captured. It was still dark and he knew nothing of the

fate of Montgomery's column. After being slightly reinforced, he shouted, "Forward, my brave fellows," and
dashed against a second battery. A detachment of British
troops met the patriots here and a terrible conflict ensued.
Morgan fought with desperation, but was forced to give
way. He attempted to cut his way through his foes, but
his numbers were too small and he was obliged to surrender.

Montgomery was but thirty-nine years of age when he
gave his life for his country on the blood-stained snows before Quebec. His career had been bright and promising
and the country mourned his loss. Montgomery was buried
by the British with the honors of war, but in 1818, the
state of New York removed his remains to New York city,
and Congress erected a monument to his bravery and
worth over them in the portico of St. Paul's Church.

PHILIP SCHUYLER.

PHILIP SCHUYLER, a major-general in the Continental army, and a close friend of Washington, was born in 1733, in Albany, New York. He received a good education, and being proficient in mathematics, embraced the profession of a civil and military engineer. The beginning of the Revolution found him rich and prosperous, but he cheerfully gave himself and his fortune to his country, and rendered incalculable aid to the cause of liberty and freedom.

Schuyler was made a major-general and placed in command of the army that invaded Canada. Falling seriously ill, he was compelled to relinquish the command to Montgomery, but upon his recovery, he conducted many difficult military operations with uncommon skill. He became especially successful in raising men for the army and money for the needs of Congress, at one time giving his personal security for a large sum of money. His energy in these transactions procured him the ill will of many who did not recognize his incorruptible honesty, and this, with other causes, induced him to resign his commission. Congress, however, in spite of the slights it had put upon him, entreated him to recall his resignation, and he did so in the cause of liberty.

While Schuyler was in command of the army operating in the North, he made all possible efforts to obstruct the

General Philip Schuyler.

march of Burgoyne and his splendid army. He tore up
bridges, cut down trees and destroyed navigation wherever possible. Consternation pervaded the country. Men,
women and children fled before the oncoming British
legions. Homes were deserted. Only the necessaries of
life were taken. Mothers aroused their sons and sent them
to face the foe. Then the battle of Oriskany was fought—
a most bloody engagement—in which the Americans were
victorious. Then Fort Schuyler was saved to the patriots.
Schuyler planned and marched and fought with consum-
mate ability, but just at the time when it seemed that he
was to reap the reward of his exertions, he was superseded,
and the command of the army given to General Horatio
Gates. Schuyler had prepared the way for the disaster
that befell Burgoyne eventually, but Gates was allowed to
receive the credit, while the man who had planned the campaign and done the hard work was pushed aside.

Schuyler witnessed the surrender of Burgoyne, but his
patriotism was of so lofty a character that not a murmur
escaped his lips when the plaudits of the nation were given
to another instead of to him, to whom they rightfully be-
longed. He made the Baroness Reidesel a guest at his own
home after the surrender, and extended his hospitality to
Burgoyne as well. Burgoyne had caused Schuyler's property at Saratoga to be burned, and this courtesy, coming
after that action, caused him to say on one occasion to
Schuyler: " You are too kind to me, who have done you so
much injury." " Oh, that was the fate of war; pray think
no more of it," was Schuyler's magnanimous reply.

Later, General Schuyler was urged by Washington to
resume the command of the army from which he had been

Burgoyne and His Indian Allies.

deposed, but he would not serve longer under the Congress which had humiliated him, and resigned from the service. He served his country, however, as a member of the New York Senate and as a member of Congress. Advancing age compelled his retirement from that body, however, and he died in November, 1804. One of his last acts was to give their freedom to all of his slaves.

BENEDICT ARNOLD.

BENEDICT ARNOLD, a major-general in the Continental army, whose incredible daring and gallant behavior in battle dazzled the American people until his treason covered his brilliant career with infamy, was born on January 3, 1740, at Norwich, Connecticut. As a boy he was noted for his love of mischief, his daring and his cruelty. It is related of him that he delighted in robbing birds' nests in order to watch the distress of the parent birds, and that he would scatter broken glass in the paths which his companions were obliged to travel barefooted. He received the best education the town afforded, and was then apprenticed to a druggist, from whom, however, he ran away when he was sixteen years of age to become a soldier. His mother, a virtuous and pious woman, was able, through friends, to effect his release, but his disposition soon induced him to run away again and join the army for the second time. Military discipline and garri-

Benedict Arnold.   91

son life were too severe for him, however, and he deserted and returned home.

After serving his apprenticeship, Arnold engaged in the business of a druggist in New Haven. In this way he acquired considerable property, which he invested in ships and entered the West India trade. After a time he became bankrupt and resumed his old business as a druggist, at the same time holding a captain's commission in a militia company. When the news of Lexington and Concord reached New Haven, Arnold found sixty men who were willing to join the patriot army with him as a leader, and with this band he marched to Cambridge, where he was soon made a colonel. When Ethan Allen moved against Fort Ticonderoga, Arnold demanded to be put in command of the expedition, but the Green Mountain Boys would have no one but Allen to lead them, and Arnold went along as a volunteer, entering the gate side by side with him. After the capture of the fort, he again claimed command, but Allen was appointed to command the garrison. His arrogance was boundless and when he was ordered to serve under another officer he flew into a rage and resigned his command.

When it was decided to send an army to invade Canada, the energy and daring of Arnold enabled him to obtain the command of ten companies of New Englanders, and three companies of riflemen, led by the celebrated Morgan. With these troops he made a march through the wilderness that was comparable with any hazardous daring in military history. Their provisions became exhausted and they were compelled to eat dogs to satisfy their hunger; they forced their rude boats across streams filled with ice: they

met and overcame perils of every description, and were
only kept from despair and death by the indomitable will
of Arnold. The worn band at last reached the walls of
Quebec and summoned the garrison to surrender. This
being refused with derision, Arnold waited for the arrival
of Montgomery. In the assault that followed, Arnold
intrepidly led his men and received a musket ball in the
leg which shattered the bone. For a time he refused to
be taken to the rear, but at last he was compelled to con-
sent.

For his bravery at Quebec, Arnold was made a brigadier-
general, and when the Americans were forced to leave Canada, he was the last man that left the territory. At the
battle of Valcour Island, he fought the British ships with
a few miserable galleys, and after a glorious fight, finding
himself no match for the enemy, he broke through the
British line, beached his galleys and set fire to them.

There is no doubt but Congress was unjust to Arnold in
the matter of promotions and in creating new major-generals. Washington felt the injustice of Congress and entreated Arnold not to act hastily in the matter. Stung to
the quick, Arnold determined to visit Congress in person.
While passing through Connecticut, he met a force of
Americans who were pursuing the British troops that had
burned Danbury. Forgetting his personal wrongs, he
joined them and participated in the fighting that followed,
exhibiting the most reckless daring and bravery. He
commanded a division at the first battle of Saratoga, and
the credit of the day is largely due to his exertions. He
burst like a whirlwind into the thickest of the fight at the
second battle near that place. His black steed was seen

wherever men fell fastest; his sword flashed wherever
death was thickest.   He led the last charge against the
British camp that ended the fight.   His horse was shot

Arnold Wounded at Battle of Saratoga.

under him, and he sank to the ground with a ghastly
wound in the same leg that was injured at Quebec.

Congress could not refuse him his rank after such
bravery.   Washington complimented him in a letter, and

later presented him with a sword and epaulettes. He was given the command of the city of Philadelphia, but he made himself unpopular. He became involved in his private affairs, and eventually he was sentenced to receive a reprimand from Washington. This he regarded as the

Capture of Andre.

crowning indignity in his career, and he began to plot treason against the government. He solicited and obtained the command of West Point and then planned to turn it over to the British. Major André was sent by Sir Henry Clinton to complete the arrangements with Arnold, and was captured within the American lines. He was tried and

executed as a spy.   Arnold escaped to the British ship
Vulture, and from there to New York.   He was made a
major-general and given a command.   He was sent to Virginia, where he laid waste the towns and devastated the
country with extreme cruelty.   Plans were formed for his
capture, but he was able to frustrate them.   At one time
he inquired of a prisoner whom he had taken, what the
Americans would do if they captured him.   The prisoner
replied, " They would cut off the leg that was wounded in
fighting for liberty and bury it with the honors of war, and
hang the rest of your body on a gibbet!"   Arnold commanded the British troops that burned New London and
Groton, and there, in his native state, apparently delighted in cruel and malignant acts.

After the close of the war Arnold went to England,
where he was given a large sum of money and received
some public favor, but he became universally detested, and
removed to St. John's, New Brunswick, where he engaged
in trade.   Afterwards he returned to England and died,
despised and shunned by all, on June 14, 1801.

Andre's Prison.

Escape of Benedict Arnold.

DANIEL MORGAN.

DANIEL MORGAN, one of the most efficient officers of the war of the Revolution, was born in New Jersey, in 1736. Nothing is known of his boyhood life, but at the age of seventeen, he is heard of in Virginia, working as a day laborer. He joined the army of General Braddock as a teamster, and on one occasion was given five hundred lashes with a whip for an alleged act of rudeness to a British officer. After Braddock's disastrous campaign Morgan was made an ensign, and on account of his judgment and bravery, was employed as a courier, going from one post to another. This service was especially hazardous, and on one occasion nearly cost Morgan his life. He and his two companions were suddenly attacked by a large party of Indians. Both his friends were killed and Morgan's jaw was shattered by a rifle ball. Clinging fast to his horse's neck, he darted away, pursued by his foes. One Indian alone was able to keep pace with the flying steed and his rider, but as he was being distanced, he threw his tomahawk, which missed its aim, and Morgan reached the nearest fort, insensible, but still clinging to his horse.

After recovering from his wound, Morgan, who was a man of splendid proportions and enormous strength, developed a love for brawls and fighting. Many of his encounters were severe, but his dogged courage always brought him victory. Eventually he settled down to the

Daniel Morgan.

life of a farmer and began to acquire property, but soon
after the battle of Bunker Hill he left his farm, enlisted a
company of riflemen, and, at their head, marched to Boston. He was attached to Arnold's command and shared
all the dangers and privations of that terrible march
through the unbroken wilderness until Quebec was
reached. He was as headlong and daring as Arnold, and
when that officer was carried to the rear, after being
wounded, Morgan took the command, and placing ladders
against the parapet poured in such a fire that the enemy
fled. When the British rallied, and their commander called
on the brave handful that was left to lay down their arms,
Morgan seized a musket, shot the officer dead, and then,
shouting " Forward, my brave fellows!" led them against
the leveled bayonets of the enemy. But his bravery and
that of his men were unavailing. They were overpowered
and forced to surrender.

Morgan's reputation was such that, during his captivity,
he was treated with kindness and offered a commission
as colonel if he would join the British army. He scorn-
fully refused the offer, and after an exchange of prisoners
was effected rejoined the Continental army. He performed splendid services at both battles of Saratoga, and
his men, with their unerring rifles, picked off the British
officers with frightful rapidity. During the first battle the
British General Frazer, mounted on a splendid gray horse,
was the soul of the British movements. Arnold instructed
Morgan not to let him remain long in the saddle. Calling
a few of his most expert marksmen to him, Morgan said,
as he pointed to Frazer: " That gallant officer is General
Frazer. I admire him, but it is necessary that he should

die. Do your duty." The third shot mortally wounded the general.

Efforts were made to prejudice Morgan against Washington, but they utterly failed, and as his health had broken down under the strain of continued active service, he obtained leave of absence to recuperate. In 1781, however, he was in South Carolina, serving under General Greene. He fought and defeated the British under Colonel Tarleton, at the battle of Cowpens, receiving a gold medal from Congress for this victory.

Morgan's riflemen were the terror of the British. The precision of their fire was marvelous. His men adored their leader, who relied more upon the affection of his men for him for effectiveness than upon discipline. He is said to have been " a fearful man in battle," and that " he fought with an obstinacy that nothing seemed able to overcome; indeed, he seldom was beaten, and even when defeated his retreat was sullen, stern and dangerous."

After Cowpens, Morgan was disabled by rheumatism and retired from the service. He died at Winchester, Virginia, on July 6, 1802.

MARQUIS De LAFAYETTE.

THE people of the United States revere the memory of the Marquis de Lafayette, a wealthy nobleman of France, who abandoned a life of luxurious ease to devote his life, his energies and his fortune to the cause of a brave people struggling to throw off oppression and exercise their heaven-born right to independence.

Lafayette was born September 6, 1757, at the Castle of Chavaniac, the ancestral home of his mother's family, in the province of Auvergne. He was the descendant of an ancient family which had furnished distinguished soldiers to France, his father being a French colonel who fell at the battle of Minden two months before his son was born. His mother was of equally ancient lineage and a lady of great wealth.

At twelve years of age Lafayette was entered at the College du Plessis, at Paris, and while pursuing his studies there both his mother and her father died, leaving him the absolute master of a fortune of between thirty thousand and forty thousand dollars a year. At the age of fifteen years he was one of the pages of the young queen Marie Antoinette and a lieutenant of musketeers, and on April 11, 1774, he married the daughter of the Duke d'Ayen, the granddaughter of one of the most powerful families at the court of France. This alliance opened the way to a brilliant career, but the young nobleman had already studied the question of civil liberty, and when he heard of the

The Marquis De Lafayette.

103

revolt of the English colonies in America, he said: "When
I first learned the subject of this quarrel my heart espoused
warmly the cause of liberty, and I thought of nothing but
of adding also the aid of my banner."

Lafayette at once placed himself in communication with
the American embassy at Paris, and declared his intention
of fitting out a vessel at his own expense. He offered to
carry out such officers as wished to ally themselves with
the cause of the colonists, and eventually sailed from
Pasage, a Spanish port, in his own vessel—La Victoire—
on April 26, 1777, accompanied by the Baron de Kalb and
eleven other French officers. Innumerable obstacles had
been placed in the way of his leaving France. His father-
in-law had procured a letter of detention from the King,
which forbade him to leave the country; but he eluded his
guards and the French cruisers which were ordered to
intercept him, and after a voyage of some weeks reached
Georgetown, South Carolina, where he was warmly welcomed by Major Benjamin Huger.

Pausing at Charleston long enough to equip one hundred and fifty men of Moultrie's command with arms and
clothing, Lafayette hastened to Philadelphia and presented
his letters to Congress. That from our minister at Paris
contained the information that he had promised Lafayette
a commission as major-general, but Congress received him
coldly. Finally, he sent that body a note, in which he
said: "After the sacrifices I have made, I have the right
to exact two favors—one is to serve at my own expense;
the other is to serve at first as a volunteer." This had the
desired effect, and Congress gave the boy of nineteen the
promised commission. Immediately afterwards he was

Lafayette Meets Washington.

introduced to General Washington, who invited him to become a member of his military family as a volunteer aidede-camp. A deep attachment grew up between the commander-in-chief and the enthusiastic youth, which lasted during their lives.

Lafayette took part in the battle of Brandywine, and was severely wounded in the leg while endeavoring to rally the broken American lines. After recovering from this wound he served under General Greene, in New Jersey, and distinguished himself by a bold attack upon the advance guard of the enemy. This gave him a reputation, and he was assigned to the command of the Virginia militia. He shared the privations of the patriots at Valley Forge, conducted a masterly retreat at Barren Hill, and fought gallantly at Monmouth, winning the thanks of Congress for his services. Later he was sent to Rhode Island to coöperate with a French fleet that had been sent to aid the patriots; and when the commander of the fleet took his ships to Boston to repair the damages inflicted by severe storms, Lafayette hurried after him to induce his return before the Americans were cut off by the reinforced British army.

In January, 1779, Lafayette sailed for France, having received leave of absence from Congress. Largely by his representations the French Government sent a force of about four thousand men to assist the American army, and after arranging for their landing Lafayette joined Washington, and was a member of the board of officers that decided the case of Major André.

He distinguished himself at the siege of Yorktown, that resulted in the surrender of Lord Cornwallis, capturing a redoubt by a headlong bayonet charge. Again obtaining leave of absence, Lafayette arrived in France in 1782, and was received with popular enthusiasm. The King conferred the rank of marshal upon him. He faithfully served the United States by raising a loan in France and later in the conduct of the peace negotiations. When the treaty was signed, he chartered a ship and despatched the first news of the event to the United States.

In 1784, Lafayette revisited America, arriving in New York on August 4. He received an ovation in every city that he visited. " In every town and village through which he passed, the mothers and daughters and widows of the land, as well as his comrades-in-arms, gathered around him with heartfelt welcome. Congress appointed committees to receive him and to bid him adieu, and in every way a grateful nation showered upon him the most gratifying marks of their love and respect." He visited his old battlefields, and was the guest of Washington, for two weeks, at Mount Vernon. Returning to France, after taking leave of Congress, he labored for the liberty of his countrymen. He passed through the terrible days of the French Revolution, refusing every offer tendered him by the monarchy. Finally he was obliged to fly from France, and falling into the hands of the Austrians, was made a prisoner. By them and the Prussian government he was treated with inhuman severity. After seeking his release in vain, his heroic wife asked the privilege of sharing his confinement. This was granted; but when her health gave way she was refused absence from her husband for the purpose of restoring it, except upon the condition that she would never return. She remained. The Emperor Napoleon I. secured the release of Lafayette and made him a peer of the realm, which dignity he refused, however, but accepted a position in the Chamber of Deputies. He also refused the cross of the Legion of Honor.

In 1824, Lafayette again visited the United States as the guest of the Nation. He was regarded as the hero of two continents, and treated everywhere with reverence and gratitude. Cities were illuminated in honor of the "people's friend," and courtesies of every kind were showered upon him. He visited the tomb of Washington, and after a magnificent reception at Yorktown passed through the principal cities of the South. Upon his return to the East he attended the laying of the corner-stone of Bunker Hill monument, performing that office with his own hands. Before he embarked for France Congress passed a bill appropriating two hundred thousand dollars and a township of land in part payment for the money he had expended in behalf of the infant republic. Upon his return to his native country he again served in the chamber of Deputies, and, in 1832, was placed in command of the National Guard. After the Duke of Orleans was proclaimed King of France Lafayette retired to private life. He died May 30, 1834.

Lafayette Laying Cornerstone of the Bunker Hill Monument.

ANDREW JACKSON.

ANDREW JACKSON, the Hero of New Orleans, and the seventh President of the United States, was born on March 15, 1767, at Waxhaw Settlement, North Carolina. His father died when Andrew was an infant, but his mother, who was a woman of uncommon strength of character, provided for her children by her own exertions and contrived to send Andrew to the best school the neighborhood afforded.

" Reading, writing and arithmetic were all the branches taught in that early day. Among a crowd of urchins, seated on the slab benches of a school like this, fancy a tall, slender boy, with bright blue eyes, a freckled face, an abundance of hair, and clad in coarse copper-colored cloth, with bare feet dangling and kicking, and you have in your mind's eye a picture of ' Andy ' as he appeared in his old field school days in the Waxhaw Settlement."

Jackson was a mischievous boy, daring, reckless and generous to a fault; fond of athletic sports, and, on the whole, " difficult to get along with." When about thirteen years of age, a number of settlers, among whom were Andrew and his brother Robert, were surprised and attacked by British and Tories in a house where they had met to defend their homes. The house was pillaged, and a British officer insolently commanded Andrew to clean boots. The boy indignantly refused and the officer struck at him with his sword. Andrew parried the blow with his

General Andrew Jackson.

left hand, receiving a cut the scar of which he carried with him through life. Robert was then ordered to clean the boots. He refused to do it and received a cut on the head from the officer's sword which eventually proved fatal.

Jackson's mother died when he was about sixteen years of age, and from that time the young man had to make his own way in life. He worked for a while in a saddler's shop, and afterwards taught school, studying law at the same time. Before he was twenty years old he practiced law. Later he moved to that section of country that eventually became the state of Tennessee, became its first member of Congress, then a member of the Senate, next a judge of the Supreme Court, and then a major-general of the state militia. In 1813, he raised a volunteer force and marched against the Creek Indians. He conquered them so thoroughly that he was made a major-general in the United States army in recognition of his services. In the latter part of 1814 Jackson was at New Orleans, after capturing Pensacola from the Spaniards, who were then assisting the British in their operations along the Gulf.

England was determined to capture New Orleans, and as their war with Napoleon was now over, it was possible to send a great and victorious army across the ocean to whip the Yankees. Thousands of veteran soldiers, trained in all the arts of war and having experiences on many a hard fought battle-field, were commanded by a brilliant leader—General Pakenham. On the same day that this proud and confident army reached the Mississippi, Jackson marched into New Orleans at the head of some strange looking backwoodsmen from Tennessee, clothed in buckskin, wearing coonskin caps and carrying long rifles.

They had fought with Indians and now were to try their strength with the trained military of the old world.

Atrocities of the Creek Indians.

Jackson had but little time in which to act. He rapidly threw up defences of mud and logs and cotton bales, and

8

when Pakenham failed to batter them down, he determined to carry them by assault. Pakenham had over ten thousand men; Jackson had less than five thousand. As the red-coated grenadiers, supported by the Scotch Highlanders in national costume, advanced upon the American fortifications, they were met by a terrific fire from the artillery, but swept on. Then the Americans arose from behind their breastworks, and, with deadly aim, poured volley after volley into the approaching lines. The carnage was awful and the British broke, only to be reformed and again hurled against the merciless fire of the frontiersmen. Again they broke and ran. Pakenham was struck by a bullet and fell from his horse; other officers took command, and they, too, were stricken down. Nothing could stay the panic; nothing could stand before the long rifles of Jackson's sharpshooters, and the British fled to the river shore, where they remained for a week, and then, leaving their cannon behind them, sailed for home. Seven hundred British were killed, fourteen hundred were wounded and five hundred taken prisoners. The American loss was seven men killed and six wounded.

In 1828, Jackson was elected President and proved to be one of the most popular men who have held that office. He served two terms and then retired to his estate, called the "Hermitage," near Nashville, Tennessee, where he died on June 8, 1845.

The Desperate British Charge at New Orleans.

115

SAM HOUSTON.

THIS distinguished soldier and quaint American character came of sturdy Scotch lineage. He was born at Timber Ridge Church, near Lexington, Rockbridge County, Virginia, March 2, 1793. His father, Major Houston, served in the Revolutionary War, and after his death, which took place when Sam was but a boy, his mother emigrated to Tennessee and settled in Blount County. Sam had but little schooling in Virginia, and not much more in his new home. It is said that he obtained from some source a copy of Homer's Iliad, and that he studied it until he could repeat it from beginning to end. He early manifested an unconquerable spirit of independence. He refused to be called by his name of Samuel and insisted upon being addressed as plain Sam. He also invariably signed his name in that way to the end of his days.

Sam became a clerk in a trader's store, but soon ran away and lived with the Cherokee Indians. He thirsted for freedom and found it in a free and untrammeled life with this tribe. In his own words, he "preferred measuring deer tracks to tape," and that "the wild liberty of the red man was more to his liking than the tyranny of his brothers." To pay a few debts that he had contracted, Houston returned to comparative civilization for awhile, and taught school to acquire the necessary money.

General Sam Houston.

When he was twenty years of age he enlisted in a Tennessee Volunteer regiment and became a splendid soldier and a fine drillmaster. He reached the grade of ensign, and fought under General Jackson at the battle of Tallapoosa. In this stubborn engagement. Houston proved himself a hero, and was severely wounded by an arrow. He also received two bullets in his right shoulder. His wounds were so severe that his recovery occupied a long time. After the peace with the Creek nation he became an agent to treat with the Cherokees, and took a delegation of them to Washington. Feeling that his services had received but slight recognition from the government, he returned home, resigned his commission, and went to Nashville to study law. His progress was so rapid that he was soon admitted to the bar. He became district attorney and made great strides in his profession. He was made a major-general of the state and was elected to Congress. In 1827, he was elected Governor of Tennessee. Later, his wife left him for a cause that has never been explained, and Houston, deeply wounded by the use his enemies made of the occurrence, resigned his office and took up his abode with his former friends, the Cherokee Indians.

Houston was formally adopted by the tribe and resumed his old name among them of the " Raven." He participated in their councils and visited Washington in their behalf in 1830, and again in 1832. He thrashed a Congressman named Stanberry and was reprimanded mildly by Congress. He was convicted of assault and battery by the criminal court and fined five hundred dollars, which fine was remitted by President Jackson. Upon his return to Tennessee he received an ovation.

The Texas Rangers at San Jacinto.

In 1834, Texas was a part of Mexico. Houston had emigrated there, and with others desired to throw off the yoke of Mexico and set up an independent republic. Houston was the leader and soul of the movement. A convention declared Texas independent, and Santa Anna, the President of the Mexican Republic, underwent a crushing defeat at San Jacinto, on April 21, 1836, on which occasion the Texans were commanded by General Houston.

Previous to this, the celebrated massacre of the Alamo had taken place. A few devoted Texans had taken refuge in an old church and were besieged by an overwhelming force of Mexicans. Travis, their gallant commander, did all that mortal man could do to strengthen the place. The enemy made two unsuccessful attempts to scale the walls. On the third attempt, the Texans, whose ammunition was then exhausted, were overpowered. " With clubbed guns the survivors fought on until nearly the whole number were cut down. Travis fell near the western wall; Crockett in a corner near the church. Bowie was butchered and mutilated on his sick-bed. Evans was shot while attempting to fire the magazine, a duty which, by agreement among the defenders, had fallen to him as the survivor. There had been no surrender; there had been no retreat. One brief hour after the Sabbath sun had touched the grim walls flying the flag of the Lone Star Republic, the sacrifice for country was complete."

At San Jacinto, Houston had only half as many men as were opposed to him, but the Texans were fighting for their liberty and won a glorious victory. Santa Anna was captured and forced to sign a treaty by which Texas was made independent. Houston had several horses shot under him and his ankle was shattered by a bullet. In this battle the watchword of the Texans was " Remember the Alamo!" and well they avenged their martyred dead.

Houston naturally received the highest honors the new republic could pay him. He was elected President, and served two terms. He ruled wisely, made treaties with warlike Indians, and eventually succeeded in having Texas admitted into the Union. Afterwards he became a United States Senator, and then Governor of the new state. He died at Huntersville, Texas, July 25, 1863.

ZACHARY TAYLOR.

ZACHARY TAYLOR, a distinguished general, and twelfth President of the United States, was born in Orange County, Virginia, November 24, 1784. His boyhood was passed upon his father's farm and in acquiring an education at the common schools of the neighborhood. When he was twenty-four years of age, his brother, Hancock, died. He had held a lieutenant's commission in the army and Zachary now applied for it. It was given to him. Two years later, he was made a captain, and in 1812 he was promoted to the rank of major for his brave defense of Fort Harrison against the Indian chief, Tecumseh.

As the settlers moved further westward, their farms and villages encroached upon the Indian border-line. The

Indians resented the presence of the white man on their lands and their great chief, Tecumseh, formed a league against the whites. He selected Fort Harrison as a point of attack, and on September 12, 1812, having failed to gain the fort by strategy, commenced a furious assault upon the

Tecumseh.

works. A little before midnight, the American sentries gave the alarm, and soon the block-house was in flames. Without were four hundred savages, led by their wily chief; inside the stockade were but fifty men, of whom two-thirds of the number were disabled by sickness. The

Zachary Taylor.

scene was one of wild confusion, but Taylor ordered the
burning boards stripped from the building, and then
earthworks were thrown up, behind which, for seven hours,
the little garrison offered such a determined resistance
that the savages were driven away.

In 1814, Taylor was fighting the combined British and
Indian forces on Rock River. In 1819, he was a lieutenant-colonel at New Orleans. He was made a colonel in
1832. He served in the Black Hawk war, and then, in
1837, he was sent against the refractory Seminole Indians,
whom he fought so successfully that the conduct of the
campaign was placed in his hands. Osceola, the chief of
the Seminoles, had gathered his braves on the edge of
a dense swamp near Lake Okeechobee, on December 25,
1837. Taylor's men charged across the morass that separated them from the foe and fought the battle knee-deep
in the wet, yielding soil. Again and again the Seminoles
threw themselves upon the foe, but nothing could break
the unflinching column before which they were obliged to
retire.

Taylor became a brigadier-general by brevet after the
battle, and was then ordered to the Southwest. The
Mexican war broke out, and on May 7, 1846, he fought the
battle of Palo Alto. He had but twenty-three hundred
men to oppose to a Mexican force of six thousand. The
battle opened with artillery and raged furiously. The
prairie grass became ignited and dense clouds of smoke
obscured both friend and foe. Then the Mexican infantry and cavalry advanced, but recoiled and fled. The next
day the Mexicans were again routed at Resaca de la Palma.
On that day, seventeen hundred men put to flight six

General Taylor at Buena Vista, Mexico.

thousand Mexicans. In June, Taylor was promoted to the rank of major-general. In the following September he captured Monterey, after a ten days' siege and three days' hard fighting. Then followed the battle of Buena Vista, where Taylor fought an army four times the size of his own.

Before the engagement the Mexican commander sent a flag of truce with a summons to surrender. Taylor knew the odds that were against him, but the message he sent back was: "General Taylor never surrenders." Then he turned to his men and said: "I intend to stand here not only so long as a man remains, but so long as a piece of a man is left." In the battle that ensued Taylor gave his celebrated order : "A little more grape, Captain Bragg." The battle of Buena Vista was a brilliant conflict, and a splendid victory for the Americans.

Taylor was beloved by his soldiers, who spoke of him as "Old Rough and Ready." He was strict in discipline, but careless about his personal appearance. He seldom appeared in uniform, and might easily have been mistaken for a farmer.

In November, 1847, Taylor asked permission to return to the United States, tiring of the inactive life he was compelled to lead after Buena Vista. He was received with enthusiastic demonstrations everywhere, and was the recipient of many flattering courtesies. Wherever he went the people made a jubilee. He was elected President in 1848, but did not live to finish his term of office. His death occurred on July 9, 1850.

WINFIELD SCOTT.

T HIS distinguished general was born on June 13, 1786, at Petersburg, Virginia. At an early age he studied law and was admitted to the bar, but in 1808, left his profession for that of a soldier, becoming a captain of light artillery. When war with Great Britain broke out, in 1812, Scott was made a lieutenant-colonel in the Second Artillery. He was among the officers at the battle of Queenstown, on the Niagara River, who displayed conspicuous skill and courage. Early in the battle the Americans were victorious, but reinforcements arrived for the British and the American army was captured. After Scott was exchanged he was made a brigadier-general. He captured Fort Erie and tore down the British flag with his own hands. On July 5, 1814, he fought the battle of Chippewa and defeated the British. Although General Brown was his commanding officer, Scott was the one who won the day, his superior saying, "To him more than any other man I am indebted for the victory."

On July 25, the battle of Lundy's Lane was fought and was a victory for the Americans. Scott had two horses killed under him, and was wounded in the right shoulder by a musket ball. Six months later peace was declared, but previous to this event Scott had been thanked by Congress, "For his universal good conduct throughout the war." After the war Scott was made a major-general and

presented with a gold medal by Congress. Later he was
sent to Europe on a confidential mission, and upon his
return was placed in command of the seaboard. For the
next thirty years he held several important positions, and
in 1841 was made commander-in-chief of the United
States army.

When the Mexican war began, General Scott arrived at
Vera Cruz and invested it on March 13, 1847. He bombarded it for fifteen days, and then the Stars and Stripes re-
placed the Mexican flag over the city and the famous fort-
ress of San Juan d'Ulloa. Scott then marched toward
the city of Mexico, and on April 18 won the battle of Cerro
Gordo. This was a hard-fought field and General Santa
Anna, who, before the battle, had boasted that he would
die fighting rather than yield, was glad to escape on a
mule, leaving his papers and his wooden leg behind him.

After Cerro Gordo, Scott pushed on, and in succession
captured Jalapa, Perote and Puebla. In two months he
had gained a series of brilliant victories and carried dismay into the very heart of Mexico. The battles of Con-
treras and Cherubusco followed, and in each instance the
Americans were victorious. Then San Antonio was captured, and but few positions lay between the invaders and
the metropolis of Mexico itself. On September 8, the for
tifications called El Molino del Rey (the King's Mills)
were carried after a desperate conflict. On the same day,
the Casa de Mata, another of the outer defenses of Chapultepec, was also stormed and carried, and the Castle
itself, situated on a rocky height, was the only obstacle
to be overcome before the Americans could plant their flag
within the capital itself. On September 12, the castle of

Winfield Scott.

Chapultepec was bombarded, and on the following day it was carried by assault. The Mexican authorities now sent a deputation to General Scott and begged him to spare the city, but Scott had expended a large number of lives in reaching the metropolis and was resolved to humble the pride of the enemy by entering in force. This he did on September 14, and the flag of the United States was raised upon the National Palace as he rode in full uniform into the Plaza, amid tremendous cheers that broke from the ranks.

Scott was given a magnificent reception upon his return to the United States, and all united to do him honor. In 1852, he was a candidate for the Presidency, but was defeated. When the Civil War broke out Scott was still the commander-in-chief of the army, but the once splendid soldier was now old and infirm. He retired to West Point, where his death occurred on May 29, 1866.

ULYSSES S. GRANT.

THIS distinguished general and afterwards the eight-
eenth President of the United States, was born on
April 27, 1822, at Point Pleasant, Clermont County,
Ohio. His ancestors distinguished themselves in the old
Scottish wars and were ever strong fighters for the cause

of liberty. Ulysses' father was Jesse R. Grant, descended
from one Matthew Grant, who came to America in 1630.
He married Miss Hannah Simpson, a native of Montgomery County, Pennsylvania, and followed the business
of a tanner.   Their son Ulysses was christened Hiram
Ulysses Grant, but the member of Congress who appointed
the boy to a cadetship at West Point, by accident changed
the name to U. S. Grant.

It is said of Grant that he never liked the business of
a tanner.   He was willing to become a farmer or follow
almost any other occupation.   He was a cool, robust, and
strong boy, neither precocious nor stupid.   After his son
had become famous, his father furnished these anecdotes
of his childhood:

"The leading passion of Ulysses, almost from the time
he could go alone, was for horses.   The first time he ever
drove a horse alone, he was about seven and a half years
old.   I had gone away from home to Ripley, twelve miles
off.   I went in the morning and did not get back until
night.   I owned, at that time, a three-year-old colt, which
had been ridden under the saddle to carry the mail, but
had never had a collar on.   While I was gone, Ulysses
got the colt and put a collar and the harness onto him,
and hitched him up to a sled.   Then he put a single line
onto him, drove off, loaded up the sled with brush, and came
back again.   He kept at it, hauling successive loads all
day, and when I came home at night, he had a pile of
brush as big as a cabin.   At about ten years of age, he
used to drive a pair of horses alone from Georgetown,
where we lived, forty miles to Cincinnati, and drive back
a load of passengers.

" When Ulysses was a boy, if a circus or any show came along in which there was a call for somebody to come forward and ride a pony, he was always the one to present himself, and whatever he undertook to ride, he rode. This practice he kept up until he got to be so large that he was ashamed to ride a pony. Once, when he was a boy, a show came along in which there was a mischievous pony, trained to go around the ring like lightning, and he was expected to throw any boy that attempted to ride him. ' Will any boy come forward and ride this pony?' shouted the ringmaster. Ulysses stepped forward and mounted the pony. The performance began. Round and round the ring went the pony, faster and faster, making the greatest effort to dismount the rider, but Ulysses sat as steadily as if he had grown to the pony's back. Presently out came a large monkey, and sprang up behind Ulysses. The people set up a great shout of laughter, and on the pony ran, but it all produced no effect on the rider. Then the ringmaster made the monkey jump up onto Ulysses' shoulders. It stood with its feet on his shoulders and with his hands holding on to his hair. At this there was another and a louder shout, but not a muscle of Ulysses' face moved. A few more turns, and the ringmaster gave it up; he had come across a boy that the pony and the monkey both could not dismount."

Grant received an education at West Point that fitted him for his work in life. He graduated in 1843, standing twenty-first in a class of thirty-nine. At West Point he was said to be a " plain, common-sense, straightforward youth, shunning notoriety, taking to his military duties in a very business-like manner—not a prominent man in the corps, but respected by all, and very popular with friends. His best standing was in the mathematical branches, and their application to tactics and military engineering."

Bombardment of Fort Sumter.

After graduating from West Point, Grant served bravely in the war with Mexico, winning the approval of his superior officers for distinguished gallantry under fire, and reaching the rank of a captain. He resigned from the army in 1854 and retired to a farm near St. Louis. In 1859 he entered into partnership with his father in the leather business, at Galena, Illinois. When Fort Sumter

Grant Captures Fort Donelson.

was fired on by the Confederates, he said to a friend: "The government educated me for the army. What I am I owe to my country. I have served her through one war, and, live or die, will serve her through this." He raised a company of volunteers at once, and tendered his and their services to the Governor of Illinois, who at once made him adjutant-general of the St te.   He rendered efficient services in this position, and was then made a

Capture of the Works at Petersburg.

colonel of an Illinois regiment, his commission dating June 15, 1861. In August of the same year he was made a brigadier-general, and in December was appointed commander of the department of Cairo. He captured Fort

Battle of Shiloh (April 7, 1862).

Henry, on the Tennessee River, and then Fort Donelson, on the Cumberland River, acting in connection with the Union gunboats. Both of them were brilliant affairs, and Grant was made a major-general.

Grant fought the great battle of Shiloh, on April 7, 1862, and in a two days' fight routed the enemy. On September 19, he fought and won the battle of Iuka, and then besieged Vicksburg. This stronghold of the Confederacy surrendered to him on July 4, 1863. In November of the same year he won a victory at Chattanooga over General Bragg. On March 1, 1864, General Grant was made lieutenant-general and commander of all the armies of the United States. Previous to this, however, Congress had voted him a gold medal for his services.

House Where Lee Surrendered.

Then Grant planned his last great campaign, and the battles of the Wilderness, Spottsylvania and Cold Harbor followed. He then besieged Petersburg and took it, and then Richmond fell into his hands. He then compelled General Lee and his whole army to surrender at Appomattox Court House, and the great Civil War was over. On July 25, 1866, Congress created the rank of General and conferred it upon Grant. In 1868 he was elected President of the United States, and again in 1872. After his second term he spent several years in a voyage around the world—one of the most memorable, in many respects, ever known in history. No man ever traveled so far and was received with such distinguished consideration wherever he went. General Grant made his home at Galena, Illinois, after his return from his tour, and later took up his residence in New York city. A cancerous affliction of the throat now seized upon him, and on June 16, 1885, he was removed to Mt. McGregor, New York, where he died on July 23, 1885.

The entire country went into mourning. Flags were at half-mast throughout the land. On August 8 the last sad rites were paid to the dead hero, and he was laid to rest at Riverside Park, New York.

WILLIAM T. SHERMAN.

WILLIAM TECUMSEH SHERMAN was born on February 8, 1820, at Lancaster, Ohio. His father died when he was nine years of age, and the boy was adopted by the Hon. Thomas Ewing, who placed him at school, where he remained until he was sixteen years old. Mr. Ewing then sent him to the United States Military Academy, at West Point, where he graduated four years later, the sixth in his class.

When Mr. Ewing offered to adopt one of the Sherman children—there were eleven of them—after the death of their father, the question arose which one he should select. "I must have the smartest of the lot," said Mr. Ewing. "Well, come and look at them and take your pick," replied the mother. Still undecided, Mr. Ewing continued: "They all look alike to me." "Take 'Cump,'" said the mother and her oldest daughter; "he's by far the smartest." In after life General Sherman said of his benefactor: "He ever after treated me as his own son." And of Sherman as a boy, Mr. Ewing said: "There was nothing especially remarkable about him, excepting that I never knew so young a boy who could do an errand so correctly and promptly as he did. He was transparently honest, faithful and reliable, studious and correct in his habits; his progress in education was steady and substantial."

According to his own account of himself, Sherman was not selected for any office at West Point, but remained a private throughout the whole four years. After his graduation he was made a second lieutenant in the Third Artillery. He served in various parts of the country until 1853, when, becoming tired of the monotony of garrison life, he resigned his commission and engaged in the banking business at San Francisco. In 1860 he became the president of the Louisiana State Military Academy, but resigned when he saw that the Civil War was inevitable.

General William Tecumseh Sherman.

When the conflict began Sherman was made a colonel, and at the battle of Bull Run commanded a brigade. In this battle he saved General Hunter's command from annihilation. Sherman was at Fort Donelson, and under Grant

Battle at Chattanooga.

at the bloody battle of Shiloh. Several horses were killed under him at Shiloh, but he seemed to bear a charmed life, although in the hottest of the fire. Grant said of him: "To his individual efforts I am indebted for the success of this battle."

Sherman at Siege of Vicksburg.

After Shiloh, Sherman was made a major-general. He was conspicuous at the siege of Vicksburg and at the battle of Chattanooga. Early in 1864 he marched towards Meridian, Mississippi, and the Confederates everywhere retreated before him. Arrived at Meridian, he burned the arsenal and many other buildings. He sent out raiding parties in every direction and destroyed everything that would benefit the Confederacy. No private property was molested, however, but it was impossible to prevent the soldiers from occasionally raiding a henroost. One who was with the army said: "An ardent secession lady discovered a vile Yankee purloining a pair of fat chickens. Terribly incensed at this wanton robbery, she made a bold onslaught, but all her expostulations failed to convince the demoralized and hungry 'mudsill' that he was sinning, for he replied, 'Madam! this accursed rebellion must be crushed, if it takes every chicken in Mississippi.'"

Sherman now invaded Georgia and defeated Generals Johnston and Hood, and besieged Atlanta. In November, 1864, Sherman began his famous march to the sea. For a time the North had no intelligence from Sherman's army. "Marching Through Georgia" has been celebrated in song and story. There were no armies to oppose the Union forces, and there were few conflicts with the people. The army foraged on a gigantic scale, but there was no pillaging. At last, Fort McAllister, near the city of Savannah, was reached. Sherman watched the assault from the roof of a mill. To General Howard, who stood by his side, he said: "See that flag in the advance, Howard? How steadily it moves. Not a man falters. There they go still. Grand! grand! That flag still goes for-

An Incident of Sherman's March.

ward! There is no flinching there! Look! It has halted! They waver—no, it's the parapet! There they go again. Now they reach it. Some are over! Look there! a flag on the works! Another! another! It's ours—the fort is ours!"

The triumphant march to the sea was ended at Savannah. After capturing the city, Sherman telegraphed to President Lincoln: "I beg to present to you as a Christmas gift the city of Savannah, with one hundred and fifty guns and plenty of ammunition, and about twenty-five thousand bales of cotton."

Sherman was made lieutenant-general in 1866, and general in 1869. He afterwards traveled abroad, and was retired from active service in 1884. His death occurred in the city of New York, on February 14, 1891.

PHILIP H. SHERIDAN.

PHILIP HENRY SHERIDAN was born at Somerset, Ohio, March 6, 1831. He was the son of Irish parents, poor as to this world's goods, and very little is known of him up to the time he was seventeen years of age, when he was sent to West Point, where he proved to be an energetic student. He had a very quick temper, however, and his life at the United States Military Academy was marked by successive quarrels and fights in which it involved him. He graduated in 1853, and for the next eight years served in the Southwest and on the Pacific Coast. He was then made a captain and stationed at

General Philip H. Sheridan.

Jefferson Barracks, Missouri. In 1862 Sheridan was the colonel of the Second Michigan Cavalry, and after the battle of Booneville, where he displayed wonderful strategic abilities, was made a brigadier-general of volunteers.

At the battle of Murfreesboro Sheridan added to his fame as a cavalry leader. General Rosecrans said in his report of that battle: " The constancy and steadfastness of his troops enabled the reserve to reach the right of our army in time to turn the tide of battle, and changed a threatened rout into a victory. He has fairly won promotion."

" Little Phil," as he was called in the army, fought with daring, skill and energy at Chickamauga and at Missionary Ridge, and later General Grant gave him the command of all the cavalry of the Army of the Potomac.

In July, 1864, the Confederate General Early invaded Pennsylvania, and burned the town of Chambersburg, contriving to elude the forces that were sent against him. Then Sheridan was placed in command and defeated him at Opequan, on September 19, and again on October 19, at Cedar Creek. Sheridan had gone to Washington, leaving General Wright in temporary command, and Early's assault, when it came, was delivered simultaneously against the front and rear. Most of the pickets were captured; the rest of the troops, suddenly aroused from sleep, were thrown into confusion and driven back towards Middletown. Eighteen of the Union guns were seized by Early and turned on their late possessors, and for a time it seemed as if the Union troops would be utterly overwhelmed. Wright formed a new line of battle, however, and kept up a desperate struggle for five hours, but his

Sheridan's Famous Ride.

lines were retreating when Sheridan rode up, having come from Winchester, thirty miles away. For two hours he rode back and forth along the line, shouting: "Face the other way, boys! face the other way! We are going back to our camp! We are going to lick them out of their boots." With shouts and cheers the soldiers followed him, filled with his own daring courage and enthusiasm. He threw them upon the enemy under an awful fire of artillery and musketry, and soon sent the foe flying in utter rout, winning a glorious victory and regaining the guns that had been lost in the morning.

For his "personal gallantry, military skill and just confidence in the courage and patriotism of his troops," Sheridan was promoted to the rank of major-general, on November 14. He had saved the Union cause from a crushing reverse and permanently crippled Early's army.

On April 1, 1865, Sheridan gained the battle of Five Forks. The desperate game of the Confederacy was almost played out. He saw his men starving to death, surrounded on every side. "Then Sheridan—that new, meteoric, dashing leader, who had at last waked up Virginia to a realizing sense of what Yankee cavalry could do when properly led, whipped his way through the Shenandoah, came trotting down the valley of the James, tearing canals, roads and railways into ruins as he rode, joined his great leader now reaching round the southern limits of the threatened lines, and then, one finger at a time, the failing grasp of Lee on his last position began to let go; and on the first of April Sheridan once more had shot round the now quivering flank, fought and won the brilliant battle of Five Forks, the real wind-up of the war."

Sheridan's Forces at Battle of Five Forks.

After giving him his instructions, Grant said to Sheridan: " I mean to end this business here," and Sheridan's reply was: " That's what I like to hear you say. Let us end this business here." After the splendid victory Sheridan sent word to Grant of his success, and the commander-in-chief telegraphed President Lincoln that " Sheridan had carried everything before him."

When Lee retreated from Richmond, Sheridan led the pursuit, and he was present when General Lee surrendered the gallant army of Northern Virginia. On that day Sheridan's form " was snugly buttoned in the double-breasted frock coat of a major-general, the dress he wore on all occasions in the field; his short legs were thrust deep into huge cavalry boots; his eyes were still snapping with the flame of the morning fight; his whole manner was so suggestive of the trick he had of hitching nervously forward in the saddle when things were not going to suit him, that he looked to some present as though he were still disposed to suspect some ruse, some trick, and was ready to spring to horse and pitch in again at an instant's notice."

After the Civil War, Sheridan commanded several military departments and was made lieutenant-general in 1869. He was made commander-in-chief of all the United States armies upon the retirement of General Sherman, and reached the full rank of general on June 1, 1888. He died on August 5, 1888, at the age of fifty-seven years. His remains were buried in the Arlington National Cemetery, and were followed to their resting place by representatives from every branch of government and by an immense concourse of private mourners.

GEORGE B. McCLELLAN.

EORGE BRINTON McCLELLAN was born in Philadelphia, Pennsylvania, September 3, 1826. His father was a physician and the boy remained under his roof until, at a proper age, he was sent to West Point. He graduated in 1846, the second in his class. He was made a second lieutenant, and soon afterwards was sent to Mexico, where he distinguished himself throughout the war. Here he developed that magnetic attraction which won him so many devoted followers among his soldiers, then and in after life. He was cool under fire at Cerro Gordo and at Chapultepec, as well as in earlier engagements, and was commended by his superior officers for " gallant and meritorious conduct."

After the close of the war with Mexico, McClellan was intrusted with various engineering expeditions, and later was instructed by the Government to investigate the entire railroad system of the United States. His report was a model of clearness and gave him a high reputation. After executing a secret mission for the Government in the West Indies, McClellan was sent to Europe, with two other army officers, to study the European armies in the Crimea. The report of this commission led to great changes in fortifications and military and naval equipment in the United States. In 1857, McClellan resigned from the army and became superintendent and afterwards president of the Illinois Central Railroad.

When the Civil War broke out, McClellan was employed by the Governor of Ohio to organize the troops from that state, and on May 13, 1861, he was assigned to the com-

Battle of Malvern Hill.

mand of the Department of the Ohio. Two campaigns in Western Virginia followed, in which he was very successful, receiving the thanks of Congress. In 1861, he

General George B. McClellan.

was relieved of his command and given that of the Army of the Potomac, a body of troops which soon assumed shape under the effects of his superb discipline. In this work he displayed rare genius and great organizing qualities.

McClellan marched towards Richmond; captured York-town; fought many battles on the Chickahominy, and then whipped the Confederate General Lee at Malvern Hill. Previous to this engagement, McClellan's operations had been severely criticized by the public and the press. It seemed as though the patience of the country was exhausted by the failure of the Army of the Potomac to accomplish anything tangible, and the people were exasperated at the severe losses that the Confederates had inflicted upon that splendid body of troops. President Lincoln telegraphed to McClellan, "I think the time is near when you must either attack Richmond or give up the job and come to the defence of Washington."

On June 30, 1862, McClellan found himself in possession of Malvern Hill. Not content with this strong position, he left the army there, and on the gunboat Galena searched for a place on the river which would be the " final location of the army and its depots." In his absence, the battle of Malvern Hill was fought; but the Confederate Army, under General Lee, was beaten back. McClellan did not follow up this decisive victory, however, but fell back to Harrison's Landing. McClellan's most devoted adherents were dissatisfied and even indignant at this policy.

In August, McClellan marched to the Potomac to resist the Confederates who had invaded Maryland. He fought the two days' battle of Antietam in September,

Battle of Antietam—Taking the Bridge.

157

but again delayed in following up his victory. In November, the command of the army was taken from him and given to General Burnside. After that McClellan took no part in the war.

In 1864, McClellan was nominated for the Presidency, but was defeated. He then resigned his commission in the army and passed some time in Europe. Upon his return to the United States he was employed as an engineer in several important undertakings, and was Governor of New Jersey from 1878 to 1881. His death occurred on October 29, 1885.

AMBROSE E. BURNSIDE.

AMBROSE EVERETT BURNSIDE came of Scotch ancestry. He was born on May 23, 1824, at Liberty, Indiana. He was sent to West Point, and graduated from there in 1847. He then served in New Mexico, and was made a first-lieutenant in 1852. He invented a breech-loading rifle and introduced some changes in the method of carrying infantry knapsacks. Meanwhile he had resigned his commission in the army, but four days after the first call for troops to defend the Union he was on the way to Washington as colonel of the First Rhode Island Volunteers. He commanded a brigade at the battle of Bull Run and soon afterwards was promoted to be a brigadier-general.

Burnside commanded the expedition that had for its object the capture of Newbern and Roanoke, early in 1862. On January 13, he made a splendid assault on the

Confederate works and carried them, sweeping everything before him. The victory was brilliant and decisive, and Burnside was made a major-general in consequence. Afterwards Burnside compelled the surrender of Fort Macon

General Ambrose E. Burnside.

and the city of Beaufort. Later he won the battle of South Mountain and commanded the left wing of McClellan's army at Antietam.

On November 7, 1862, McClellan surrendered the command of his army to General Burnside. Previous to this date, the position had been offered to Burnside, but had been refused. It was only on the peremptory order of the War Department that he accepted it now. Burnside reorganized the army, somewhat, and then moved on Fredericksburg, situated on the southern side of the Rappahannock, where the Confederates had posted heavy batteries. Burnside had at this time an army of one hundred and fifty thousand men and a splendid artillery train. It took him weeks to build pontoon bridges and transfer his army across the river, but it was finally accomplished and the battle of Fredericksburg began at an early hour on December 13, 1862. Burnside hoped to cut the enemy's line in two, but was unable to do so. Again and again the Union divisions were ordered to expel the Confederates from the woods and hills back of Fredericksburg at the point of the bayonet, but every assault that was made by the Union forces was beaten back by the enemy. The contest continued until dark, but the Union troops were unable to win a single yard or dislodge their opponents from their possessions. Neither army assumed the defensive on the following day, but later, Burnside, influenced by the advice of his generals, withdrew from his perilous position. Two days later Lee found nothing before him but a deserted land, a ruined town, a winding river and a line of batteries frowning from the opposite shore. The affair was disastrous to the Union cause, but Burnside took the entire responsibility of it upon himself and resigned the command of the army.

In 1863, Burnside drove the Confederates out of East Tennessee and made a brilliant entry into Knoxville, where the loyal inhabitants received him with great demonstrations of joy. His operations were successful until, in 1864, while assisting Grant before Petersburg, his secret mining operations proved a failure and the enemy were actually benefited by the explosion that was confidently expected to benefit the Union cause. Burnside proffered his resignation, but it was not accepted and a leave of absence was given him instead. He eventually resigned from the army in 1865, and the following year was elected Governor of Rhode Island. He visited Europe in 1870 and tried his hand at mediation between the powers of France and Germany, but without success. He afterwards served Rhode Island in Congress. His death took place on September 13, 1881, at Bristol, in that state.

GEORGE H. THOMAS.

GEORGE HENRY THOMAS, was born on July 31, 1816, in Southampton County, Virginia. He was the child of wealthy parents and received an excellent education. When twenty years of age, he entered the United States Military Academy at West Point, and graduated the twelfth in his class of forty-five, in 1840. He was made a second lieutenant in the Third Artillery, and his first service was against the Seminole Indians in Florida. His conduct in battle was gallant and irreproachable, and later he was stationed at Fort Moultrie, and still later at Fort McHenry. In 1845, he was in Mexico with General Taylor. He was conspicuous at the storming of Monterey and bore a distinguished part at

11

the battle of Buena Vista. After the close of the Mexican war, after performing various services at different points, he was an instructor at West Point for about three years. He then served with distinction in the West, and in 1860, asked for and obtained a short leave of absence—the first he had asked for during a service of twenty years.

Although a native of Virginia, Thomas remained faithful to the Union instead of following the fortunes of his state, and was soon in command of a brigade, with the rank of colonel. During the early part of the Civil War, he fought under Rosecrans and Grant, and in 1862 was made a major-general. He distinguished himself at Mill Spring and at Shiloh, and then commanded the post at Nashville. He became the faithful friend and adviser of his superior officers and was known as one on whom they could rely. Rosecrans gave him great credit at Murfreesboro, and then came the battle of Chickamauga, where his bold stand saved the Union army from destruction. It was his rock-like firmness that saved the army from a terrible beating and from being driven out of Tennessee. At a critical time during the battle, and when reinforcements were badly needed, Thomas sat upon his horse watching the advance of heavy columns, away to his left. Not knowing whether they were friends or foes, he raised his glass and in silence watched the advancing troops. Turning to his staff after a few moments, he said: "Take my glass, some of you whose horse is steady, and tell me what you can see." One of his officers thought he could make out the "Stars and Stripes." "Thomas caught up his glass again, and watched the advancing column with deepening anxiety. Suddenly the glass was lowered, and a load was lifted from his heart. A light wind caught the standards and flapped out every fold to its fullest extent, and the sunlight, breaking through the clouds of dust, shone on the red and blue bars and the white crescent of Gordon Granger's battle-flag." None too soon, though; but

General George H. Thomas.

Thomas held his ground as the battle ebbed and flowed, and fell back suddenly during the night, unmolested by the enemy.

Later, General Bragg invested Chattanooga, which

Thomas was holding. Grant sent word to hold out to the last. Thomas' answer was: "I will hold the town till we starve!"

In 1864, Thomas commanded the Army of the Cumberland under General Sherman. He decided the fate of Atlanta, and then Sherman left him to whip Hood and cover his rear during his march to the sea. Sherman afterwards said: "If Thomas had not whipped Hood at Nashville, six hundred miles away, my plans would have failed, and I would have been denounced the world over. But I knew General Thomas and the troops under his command and never for a moment doubted a favorable result."

Thomas' task was to improvise an army with which to repel Hood's invasion of Tennessee, and he did it. In the two days' fighting at Nashville, he completely smashed the Confederate general. After the magnificent charge of the second day, a captured Confederate general said, "Why, sir, it was the most wonderful thing I ever witnessed. I saw your men coming and held my fire—a full brigade, too—until they were in close range, could almost see the whites of their eyes, and then poured my volley right into their faces. I supposed, of course, that when the smoke lifted, your line would be broken and your men gone; but it is surprising, sir, it never staggered them. Why, they did not even come forward on a run. But right along, cool as fate, your line swung up the hill, and your men walked right up to and over my works and around my brigade before we knew they were upon us. It was astonishing, sir, such fighting."

Thomas was known to his soldiers as old " Major Slow-

Battle of Chickamauga (September 19-20, 1863).

Trot," but they worshiped him. **He received** a gold medal from the state of Tennessee for his **victory** at Nashville, **also** the thanks of Congress, and was made a major-general in the regular army. In 1868, he declined the office of lieutenant-general, saying he had done nothing **to** deserve it. His death occurred **at** San Francisco, on March 28, 1870.

JOSEPH HOOKER.

"FIGHTING JOE HOOKER," **as** he came to be called during the Peninsular campaign of the Civil War, was born at Hadley, Massachusetts, November 13, 1814. He graduated from West Point in 1837, and fought in the Florida and Mexican Wars, being three times promoted for gallant conduct. He resigned his commission in 1853, and settled down to the life of a farmer, in the West. He entered the army again in 1861, and **soon** became a brigadier-general. A year later he was promoted to be a major-general.

Hooker made himself conspicuous **for** bravery, dash, and daring throughout McClellan's operations before Richmond, and in the Maryland campaign that followed he participated actively, especially at South Mountain. He **was** wounded at Antietam and compelled to retire from the field. He commanded a division under Burnside at Fredericksburg, and succeeded to the command of the Army of the Potomac after the resignation of that general.

When Hooker assumed command of the Army of the Potomac it was in a despondent state, as was the country itself, but he succeeded in reorganizing it and took the field with a splendid force in a high state of discipline.

General Joseph Hooker.

Heavy rains and swollen streams were against him on his way to Chancellorsville, but he made his celebrated "mud march" of thirty-seven miles, encumbered with baggage and artillery, crossed two rivers and reached Chancellorsville on April 30, 1863. The bloody battle

that ensued was precipitated by the Confederate General
Jackson, who fell upon the right of Hooker's army.   The
corps that was attacked was preparing supper and arranging for the night.   Suddenly, Jackson's men made the
attack and drove the Union forces before them.   A furious conflict took place later, when Hooker attempted to
recover the field.   He was wounded and for a time was
unable to direct the operations of his troops.   His army
was divided, while that of the enemy was not, and Hooker
was obliged to retreat.   He resigned his command on June
27, 1863, and General Meade took his place.

Later in the year, Hooker was at Chattanooga, and during the "battle above the clouds," won imperishable renown.   No battle was ever like it.   The impossible was
attempted.   At the word "Forward!" the troops rushed
forward over ravines, felled trees, and rough boulders; on
and always up, lost in the clouds that wrapped Lookout
Mountain in their fleecy folds, until the foe was driven
from the summit, and the Union flag unfurled fifteen hundred feet above the Tennessee.   "At two o'clock, a glow-
ing line of lights glittered obliquely across the breast of
Lookout.   It was the Federal autograph scored along the
mountain.   They were our camp-fires.   Our wounded lay
there through all the dreary nights of rain, unrepining
and content.   Our unharmed heroes lay there upon their
arms.   Our dead lay there, 'and surely they slept well.'"

Hooker was with Sherman in his march to the sea.   His
last great contest with the Confederates was near Peach
Tree Creek, where he "bore the brunt of the shock."   He
resigned in August, 1864, when an officer inferior in rank
was promoted over him, but later he commanded different

departments in the army and was mustered out of the volunteer service in September, 1866. Two years later he was breveted major-general in the regular army and later, retired to private life. He died at Garden City, New York, on October 31, 1879.

GEORGE G. MEADE.

GEORGE WASHINGTON, the first commander-in burg," was born on December 30, 1815, at Cadiz, Spain, where his father at that time was United States consul. His grandfather was a patriotic merchant of Philadelphia, and at one time, when it was sorely needed, made the Continental Government a present of several thousand dollars. When but twenty years of age, Meade graduated from West Point, served for a while against the Indians in Florida, and then resigned his commission, becoming a civil engineer. He entered the army again in 1840, and during the Mexican War served on the staffs of both General Taylor and General Scott. The city of Philadelphia gave him a sword of honor upon his return from the campaign.

Meade engaged in the Civil War, and was made a brigadier-general after the battle of Bull Run. He was with McClellan during the Peninsular and Maryland campaigns. He especially distinguished himself at Antietam, having two horses shot under him in a headlong charge against the Confederates in the early part of the battle, in which he was wounded. In 1863, he was given the command of the Army of the Potomac, having been made a major-general previously.

In June, 1863, both the Union and Confederate armies were north of the Potomac, and the whole country held its breath as it waited for the result of the combat that must soon follow. On one side was the noble Lee, the idol of the South, with his superbly disciplined infantry; the hard riding troopers of Stuart; " Stonewall " Jackson's old command under Ewell; A. P. Hill, a most gallant officer; Long-street, with a magnificent force, including Hood's Texans, and Pickett with his Virginians. These and other gallant Confederates fought for the South in the greatest battle ever known on the continent.

Against them was Meade, a modest, faithful soldier, a man who commanded respect, and under him were Reynolds, the brilliant; the knightly Hancock; brave Sickles; Sykes, the reliable; Howard, eminent for piety; Slocum, the senior of many in rank, and scores of other brave and determined fighters.

The story of the three days of desperate fighting when the North and the South grappled at Gettysburg, requires volumes for the telling. The first day's combat opened in the forenoon of July 1. The Confederates advanced and engaged Reynolds' corps on the western side of the town. Reynolds rode forward to superintend his troops in person, but was immediately killed by a rifle bullet. The command then devolved on General Doubleday, but he was not able to check the Confederate advance. The scene of the fighting was a small open valley, consisting

General George G. Meade.

of ploughed fields, bounded by thickly wooded uplands.
Howard, riding in advance of his troops, then came up and
took command, but still the Southerners gained ground.
Then Meade sent Hancock to take the chief command, and
with Howard he formed the broken corps afresh on the
summit of the rising ground. The Confederates occupied
the town that night.

General Meade arrived at Cemetery Ridge at one o'clock
in the morning, and inspected the field. In the afternoon
the Confederates advanced, and Longstreet attacked the
Union left, commanded by Sickles. In spite of all his resistance, Sickles was driven back with terrible loss, and he
himself was severely wounded. But Meade strengthened
his lines and his guns did terrible execution, and at this
point the Southern troops were compelled to retire.
Ewell attacked Cemetery Hill and demonstrations were
made against other portions of the Union line, but these
attempts were not well supported, and the result of the
day's operations was that the Confederates were driven
back with enormous loss. Meade's troops also suffered severely.

The struggle began again on the morning of July 3,
this time on the left of the Confederate line. All the
strength of the enemy was gathered up and thrown in
one last, desperate effort on the Union forces. At half-
past twelve a furious cannonade burst from more than
one hundred guns, forming the batteries of Longstreet
and Hill. Ewell's guns were directed against the slopes
of Cemetery Hill. The Union guns blazed in reply and
for two hours the narrow valley thundered and roared with
an infernal interchange of death. Great limbs were

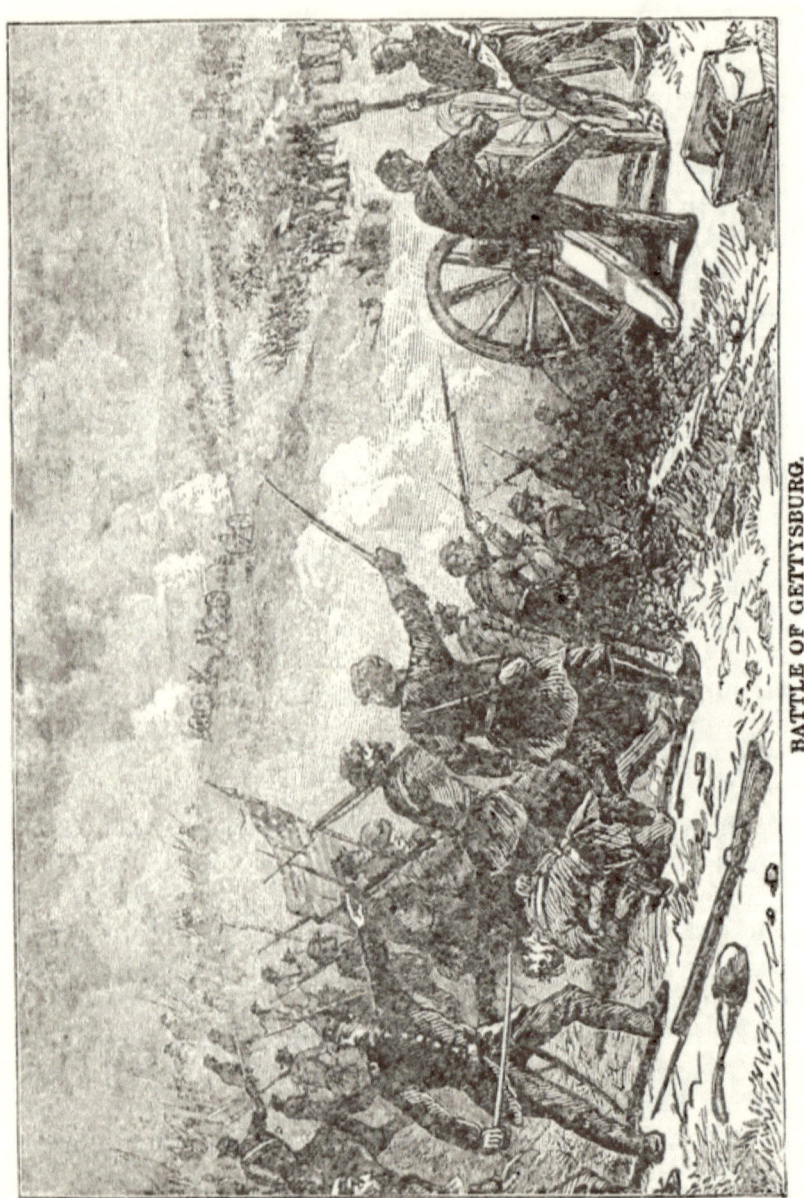

BATTLE OF GETTYSBURG.

torn from trees; rocks were splintered, and death and destruction scattered far and wide. Then Pickett's Virginians charged. In a vast, surging, gray wave, they tore up the slope and gained the crest, only to be beaten back by the blue lines blazing with fire. It was a combat of giants. Battle flags were shot to earth quicker than men could pick them up. The gray coats dropped by hundreds as regiments and brigades came to the assistance of those who defended the crest of the line, and Pickett made his way back under cover of the friendly smoke. Desultory engagements took place in other parts of the field, but the battle of Gettysburg was over and a thrill of hope ran through the North, " such as had not been known since the beginning of the long and cruel war." The tide had at last turned, but not until Virginia had ridden on the topmost wave and been dashed on the rocks of Gettysburg.

After the battle of Gettysburg, Congress promoted Meade to the rank of brigadier-general in the regular army. He remained, however, at the head of the Army of the Potomac and enjoyed the confidence of Grant, who was then Lieutenant-General of the armies. After the surrender of Lee's army, Meade was made a major-general in the regular army and later was given command of the military division of the Atlantic, with headquarters in Philadelphia. He died in that city on November 6, 1872, in a house which his gratified countrymen had presented to him.

GEORGE A. CUSTER.

GEORGE ARMSTRONG CUSTER, the dashing cavalryman whose name is everywhere associated with brave and chivalrous daring, was born on December 5th, 1839, in the little village of New Rumley, Ohio. As a boy he was a sturdy little fellow with flaxen hair, amiable in his disposition, and very fond of playing soldier. When quite young he made his home with a relative in Monroe, Michigan, and in the schools of that town acquired an education that qualified him for a successful examination to the Military Academy at West Point. He entered in 1857, made rapid progress in his studies and especially excelled in horsemanship.

After graduating from West Point, Custer reported for duty at Washington. He was at once made the bearer of despatches to General McDowell and assigned to Company G, Second Cavalry. Later he served on the staff of General Kearney. His first actual fighting was in a skirmish with a detachment of Confederates, whom he routed at the head of his company. Later, he obtained leave of absence and visited his old home at Monroe. While there he indulged some of the habits he had acquired in the field—he became intoxicated and was seen on the street in that condition. His sorrowing sister reproved him so judiciously, however, that the heart of the young man was touched. It was the turning point in his life. He made a solemn pledge not to taste a drop of intoxicating

spirit as long as he lived.   He kept his word and became
a sincere Christian.

Returning to the field, Custer performed various duties.
He served on the staff of General W. F. Smith and was
in charge of balloon reconnoissances.   On one occasion he
crossed the Chickahominy River to make observations, and
on his return, wet, muddy and untidy, was summoned to
General McClellan's presence.   They conversed for a short
time and the General offered him a place on his staff.   Custer accepted gladly and performed splendid services in that
capacity.

Many incidents are related of Custer's personal bravery
and daring.   By a dashing movement he fell upon the
celebrated "Louisiana Tigers," captured them and their
colors and returned in safety.   He served through the
Peninsular campaign and was continually performing brilliant feats.   On one occasion, he heard the young bugler
cry out, "Captain! Captain! here are two 'Secesh' after
me."   He captured one and sent him to the rear, but the
other set off with Custer after him.   The man would not
surrender, so Custer was obliged to shoot him.   His spoils
were a splendid horse, saddle and trappings, and a magnificent sword.

Custer was afterwards on General Pleasanton's staff,
and at the fight at Aldie with Stuart's cavalry he won
the star of a brigadier-general.   Kilpatrick, Douty and
Custer led the charge.   Douty was killed, Kilpatrick's
horse was shot under him, but Custer bore a charmed life
and led his men to victory.   He was afterwards made commander of the Michigan cavalry brigade.   At Gettysburg,
he charged at the head of a company and drove the enemy

12   177

before him.   When Lee surrendered, his first flag of truce was sent to Custer.

After the war, Custer, who had been mustered out as a major-general of volunteers, was, in the reorganization of the army, made lieutenant-colonel of the Seventh Cavalry, and in 1867, was sent to the plains.   He became a great hunter and had many perilous adventures fighting the Indians.   His success as an Indian fighter exceeded that of any officer in the army.   His last battle was fought on the Little Big Horn River, June 25, 1876.   By the blunders and incompetency of his subordinates, Custer found himself surrounded by swarms of Indians under Chief Rain-in-the-Face.   The heroic band made a desperate stand, but every man was killed.   Custer was the last to fall.   He was shot by Rain-in-the-Face himself, in fulfilment of a vow he had made.   All were buried on the spot where they fell and a monument to their memory was erected by the Government, bearing their names and titles.   Later Custer's remains were removed to West Point and interred in the United States cemetery.   Of Custer it has been said, " Truth and sincerity, honor and bravery, tenderness and sympathy, unassuming piety and temperance, were the mainsprings of Custer, the man."

ELMER E. ELLSWORTH.

THE pure and noble manhood of Elmer Ephraim Ellsworth and his martyrdom early in the Civil War
have endeared him to the people of the United
States. He was born on April 23, 1836, at Mechanicsville, New York. His education was acquired at common
schools. He then learned the trade of a printer and later
set up in business for himself. Through the dishonesty
of others he failed in business, but he did not complain
and began the study of law, earning a meagre living by
copying papers and documents whenever he could obtain
such employment. He had a terrible struggle with poverty, but would accept no favors or courtesies that he
feared he would be unable to return.

He is described as having a voice which was " deep and
musical, and instantly attracted attention. His form,
though slight, was very compact and commanding; the
head statuesquely poised and crowned with a luxuriance
of curling black hair; a hazel eye, bright though serene,
the eye of a gentleman as well as a soldier; a nose such as
you see on Roman medals; a light mustache just shading
the lips that were continually curving into the sunniest
smiles."

Previous to the Civil War, he became interested in
military science and developed into an enthusiast in that
direction. He saw the defects in the militia drill of the
United States, and set about demonstrating his theories.

He was a superb fencer, holding his own against the most dashing swordsmen of two worlds. He was a magnificent shot with a revolver. He organized the United States Zouave Cadets of Chicago, in 1859, clothing and drilling them according to his own ideas. " He drilled these young men for about a year, at short intervals. His discipline was very severe and rigid. The slightest exhibition of intemperance or licentiousness was punished by instant degradation and expulsion. He struck from the rolls at one time twelve of his best men for breaking the rule of total abstinence. His moral power over them was perfect and absolute. Any one of them would have died for him!" He also organized and drilled other companies at different points. He gave exhibition drills at fairs and at New York, Boston, Philadelphia and Washington. New York's crack organization was vanquished by the Ellsworth Zouaves and their fame spread throughout the country.

At one time Ellsworth studied law in the office of Abraham Lincoln at Springfield, Illinois. When the President-elect went to Washington for his inauguration, Ellsworth was among his escort. When the Civil War broke out, he rushed to New York and raised a regiment among the New York firemen. He recruited, drilled and had them in Washington within three weeks. His regiment was the idol of the public and he personally attended to every detail of regimental business.

On the night of May 23, 1861, Ellsworth and his Zouaves crossed the Potomac and entered Alexandria. His mission was to take possession of the telegraph office and to stop railroad communication. Observing the flag that

Elmer E. Ellsworth.

was flying over the Marshall House, Ellsworth entered the hotel with a detachment of his men, and asked a partially undressed man whom he met what flag it was. The man replied that he knew nothing about it. Ellsworth then ran up-stairs to the roof and cut down the flag. On his way back a man shot him in the breast with a double-barrelled gun. Private Brownell immediately shot the man, who proved to be one Jackson, the proprietor of the hotel, and the man of whom Ellsworth had inquired regarding the flag. An eye witness of the murder said: "The chaplain turned him over and I stooped and called his name aloud, at which, I think he murmured inarticulately. Winser and I lifted the body with all care, and laid it upon a bed in a room near by. The rebel flag, stained with his blood, we laid about his feet."

Ellsworth's remains were removed to Washington and laid in state in the White House. On May 25, funeral obsequies were held amid the tolling of bells and universal grief. Honors were paid the body of the young martyr in the cities through which it passed on its way to the home of his parents at Mechanicsville, where it was interred.

ROBERT E. LEE.

ROBERT EDWARD LEE, a distinguished general and the idol of the Southern Confederacy, was born on January 19, 1807, at Stratford House, in Westmoreland County, Virginia. His father was General Henry Lee, the famous "Light Horse Harry," of Revolutionary times. His mother was Matilda, daughter of Philip Ludwell Lee. No brighter name appears in American history than that of Lee. Richard Lee, an ancestor, settled in Virginia during the reign of Charles I. and occupied a prominent and honorable position in colonial affairs, and his descendants have maintained the reputation of the family name.

Young Lee was but eight years of age when the British ravaged the southern coast and burned the city of Washington. He was twelve years old when his father died, and eighteen when he entered the United States Military Academy at West Point. His conduct during his entire course at this institution was exemplary in the highest degree. He never used intoxicating liquor or tobacco; he never received a reprimand or a demerit, and he stood at the head of his class from first to last. He graduated on July 4, 1829, and was at once appointed to the corps of Topographical Engineers. He made a brilliant marriage in 1832, and in course of time two of his three sons became major-generals in the Confederate army.

Lieutenant Lee continued to follow his chosen profession, and in 1838, reached the grade of captain. He superintended many important operations in different parts of the country, and when the Mexican War broke out, was made chief of engineers under General Scott. He served in that war with distinction and was twice promoted. General Scott esteemed him highly, and in after years said: " Lee is the greatest military genius in America."

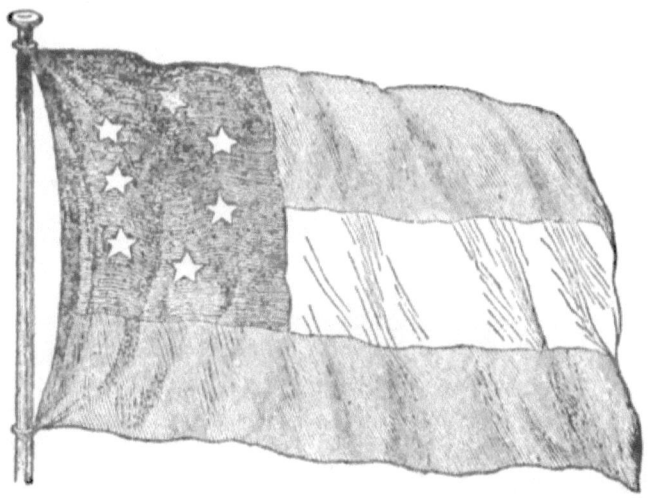

In 1852, Colonel Lee was superintendent of the Military Academy at West Point. He held this position for three years. When John Brown captured the United State arsenal at Harper's Ferry, in 1859, Lee was sent to recover the arsenal. With a detachment of marines, he attacked and captured Brown and his party, and turned them over to the civil authorities. He then served in Texas, but in 1860, was in Virginia on leave of absence.

General Robert E. Lee.

Lee early cast in his fortunes with his native state. Untiring efforts were made to retain him in the old service, but he said," How can I draw my sword upon Virginia—my native state." He resigned from the United States army April 20, 1861, and was at once appointed commander of the Virginia forces. It was not without a long and bitter struggle that he left the flag under which he had fought from early manhood, to serve under the " Stars and Bars," but he held that his first duty was to his state; she had called her children to take up arms in her defence, and her cry could not go unheeded.

For a time he held no important command, but on June 3, 1862, he was made commander of the Confederate army of Northern Virginia. This position he held throughout the war. In the same month in which he assumed command of this army, Lee administered blow after blow upon McClellan, who was opposed to him, and forced him to retreat to the James River. McClellan, however, stood his ground at Malvern Hill, and Lee's impetuous columns were beaten back at that time. Lee then joined " Stonewall " Jackson and whipped Pope on the old battlefield of Bull Run. He next invaded Maryland, and Jackson captured Harper's Ferry. Then followed the battle of Stone Mountain and the bloody field of Antietam, after which he retreated across the Potomac. At Fredericksburg, Lee administered a crushing defeat to the Union forces under Burnside, and at Chancellorsville, while he won a victory, it cost him the life of Jackson and ten thousand gallant men.

Lee's invasion of Pennsylvania resulted in the battle of Gettysburg, which was a victory for the Union forces.

General Lee Bidding Farewell to his Soldiers.

Lee withdrew up the Valley of Virginia, followed by Meade. In 1864, Grant moved towards Richmond. Lee struck him a terrible blow in the densely wooded region, known as the Wilderness. The combat was one of the bloodiest of the war, and lasted for three days, but was indecisive in its results. Lee won at Spottsylvania Court House, and repelled Grant's attack upon his entrenchments at Cold Harbor, but was compelled to retreat from Petersburg. The Confederate army was brave as ever, but was wasted by sickness and death. The South was exhausted, not beaten, and the end came at Appomattox. Lee and Grant met at a plain country house there and arranged the terms whereby the gallant army of Northern Virginia laid down its arms. Lee said to them: "We have fought through the war together. I have done the best I could for you."

After the war, General Lee became president of Washington College, Lexington, Va. His death occurred at that place October 12, 1870.

THOMAS J. JACKSON.

THOMAS JONATHAN JACKSON, commonly known as " Stonewall" Jackson, was born at Clarksburg, Va., January 21, 1824. He was left an orphan at an early age, and from then until he was seventeen years old, he worked on the farm of an uncle. He went to school when he could and studied hard. He was prompt and faithful in all his duties and won the admiration of all around him for the sterling qualities he manifested. When but sixteen years old, the people of Lewis County made him constable of the county, and in spite of his youth, he discharged the duties of the office with success.

When seventeen years of age, Jackson applied for and obtained an appointment to the United States Military Academy at West Point. He entered in 1842, studied hard, and graduated four years later with distinction. He was noted for the thorough mastery of any subject he attempted. After graduation he was appointed to the First Artillery. This regiment was then serving under General Taylor in Mexico, but Jackson did not join it in time to see service until the following year, when he participated in the siege of Vera Cruz, under General Scott. For his services there, he was promoted to a first lieutenantcy. During the campaign that resulted in the fall of the city of Mexico, Jackson so distinguished himself that he reached the rank of major—a series of promotions unequalled by any other officer in that army. After the

close of the war Jackson's health was so impaired that he
resigned his commission. In 1851, he became a professor
in the Virginia Military Institute, at Lexington, also an
instructor in artillery tactics. It is said that Major Jackson was not as popular as some of the other professors,
but he possessed the respect of his pupils. He had a
wonderful memory, and in listening to a recitation would
seldom use a book. He became an active and zealous
member of the Presbyterian Church and was honored for
his piety.

The opening of the Civil War found Jackson ready to
share the fortunes of Virginia. Like Lee, he came to the
deliberate conclusion that his state had the right to demand his services. His first duties were in drilling the
raw troops that poured into Richmond from all parts of
the state. In June, 1861, he destroyed the railroad at
Martinsburg, and later checked the advance of the Union
forces at Falling Waters. At the Battle of Bull Run,
Jackson, who was then a brigadier-general, led the advance
of Johnston's army and was slightly wounded. It was
here that Jackson gained his name of " Stonewall." He
had charged the Union lines and saved a Confederate brigade. Its leader then called to his own men: " Look yon-
der! there is Jackson standing like a stonewall. Let us
determine to die here, and we will conquer. Follow me!"
This appeal was repeated throughout the army until the
name " Stonewall " was universally applied to Jackson.
He was made a major-general after this battle, and placed
in command of the Valley of Virginia. Jackson's work
in the valley was arduous; he had to dispute the advance
of Fremont, Banks and McDowell, but the result of the

General Thomas J. Jackson (" Stonewall ").

191

operations there was that Banks was whipped at Winchester and fled across the Potomac. Large quantities of military stores fell into the hands of the Confederates.

In the Shenandoah Valley, Jackson successfully fought armies much larger than his own, and the campaign closed with the battles of Cross Keys and Port Republic. He then joined Lee and decided the battle of Cold Harbor by his timely arrival. He also took a leading part in the battles of White Oak Swamp and Malvern Hill. When Lee invaded Maryland, Jackson led the advance. He invested and captured Harper's Ferry and then took part in the terrible fight at Antietam. He commanded the right wing at Fredericksburg and beat back Franklin's corps, repulsing it with heavy loss. Jackson was conspicuous for bravery during this battle, and at one time, when the conflict was raging, he rode a short distance in front of his line; took off his hat, and with his right hand raised to heaven, prayed the God of battles to be with the army that day.

At Chancellorsville, Jackson grappled with Slocum and then proposed to Lee a movement upon Hooker's right. " Unaware of impending danger, Howard's corps was preparing supper and arranging for the night. Suddenly, with a yell that arose above the bugle calls and outpost fire, the flower of Lee's army fell upon Devens, at the extreme of the Union line. Amid the pandemonium of sound, the Unionists flew in a panic before the irresistible onrush of the Southerners. In a turbulent tide they streamed to the rear and along the road to Chancellorsville, their commander severely wounded; one third their number were captured or disabled. The contagion of panic

Jackson's Charge at Battle of Bull Run (July 21, 1861).

spread to Schurz's and Von Steinwehr's divisions; the few regiments who stood their ground crumbled before the assault of the gray-coated legions. With half their number dead or dying, they joined their flying comrades. Through the summer twilight, what was once the gallant Eleventh still fled along the dusty roads."

While reconnoitering for a second attack, Jackson and his escort were mistaken for Union cavalry and fired upon by his own men. Two of his staff were killed and Jackson received a bullet in the right hand and two in the left arm. He was carried to the rear under a fearful fire from the Union lines. One of his litter bearers was killed, and the litter fell to the ground. His arm was amputated, and after the operation he seemed to revive, but pneumonia set in, the result of exposure a few nights before. On the night in question one of his aides offered him a cape, as the general had no protection from the cold. Jackson accepted it, but in the night arose and covered the young officer with it as he lay asleep, passing the remainder of the night without covering for himself.

General Jackson died on May 10, 1863, and among his last words were, " Let us cross over the river, and rest under the shade of the trees."

NELSON A. MILES.

NELSON APPLETON MILES was born at Westminster, Massachusetts, August 8, 1839. His father was Daniel Miles, a sterling, resolute man, a descendant of Rev. John Miles, a Welsh clergyman, an Indian fighter and a schoolmaster. His grandfather and great-grandfather took part in the battles of Lexington and other engagements during the Revolutionary War. His mother, Mary Custis, was a noble Christian woman, a descendant of William Curtis, who settled in Boston in 1632.

General Miles' own account of his childhood tells us that it was an ideal one. " From my earliest recollection I have felt at home on horseback." He adds:

General Nelson A. Miles.

" I first rode in front of my father with his arms about me; afterward behind him, holding on with my arms; later alone, clinging to the mane. I was given a horse and rode him and managed him at the age of six. I became at an early age passionately fond of coasting, skating, ball-playing, swimming, hunting and trapping, and many a day was delightfully spent in exploring the surrounding country, with a favorite dog as my only companion."

Miles' education was derived from the district school in the neighborhood of his father's farm, and later at an academy. He exhibited a tendency for a military life, but no opportunity offered itself in that direction, and at sixteen years of age he engaged in mercantile pursuits in the city of Boston. He, however, found time to study military history and art and devoted a portion of his time to military drill.

Early in 1861, Miles recruited a company of volunteers, was chosen captain, commissioned by the governor of the state, and duly mustered into the United States service. He was then a smooth-faced young man of twenty-one years, eager for service against the enemies of his country. He began his military service, however, as a first lieutenant in the Twenty-second regiment of Massachusetts Volunteers, commanded by Colonel Henry Wilson, who afterwards became vice-president of the United States. The reason for his reduction in rank was that the governor recalled his commission, and gave it to a political friend, alleging Miles' youth as his reason for the acton. Miles would not abandon the service he had undertaken, and, though feeling the injustice deeply, started upon that career that brought him eventually to the proud position of general-in-chief of the armies of the United States.

In 1862, Miles was the colonel of the Sixty-first New York Volunteers; became a brigadier-general in May, 1864; a major-general the following year. He served with distinguished bravery at Williamsburg and the terrible fighting at Seven Pines, was wounded at Fair Oaks, and participated with great credit in the other battles of the Peninsular campaign. He was seriously wounded at Fredericksburg and again at Chancellorsville, where his hurt was supposed to be mortal. He recovered, however, and took an active part in the campaign of 1864 and also that of 1865. For a time, he was in command of the Second Army Corps, the largest body of men ever commanded by a young man of twenty-five years. After the Civil War, General Miles was commissioned a colonel and brevet-major-general in the regular army, and in 1869, commanded the First United States Infantry.

"Thenceforward," in his own words again, "I continued to serve west of the Missouri until the fall of 1890, a period of nearly twenty-two years." Afterwards, he was sent to Europe to observe the Turco-Grecian war as the representative of the United States, and in the same capacity was present at Queen Victoria's Diamond Jubilee, in 1897.

General Miles successfully conducted many Indian campaigns. He prevented many Indian wars by a judicious and humane settlement of difficulties, without displaying military force, and was thanked by many states and territories.

In 1898, when the United States declared war with Spain on account of the cruelties practiced by the latter nation in Cuba, General Miles was at the head of the armies of the United States. He did not take the field, however, until July 7th, when he sailed with reinforcements for the army in Cuba. He arrived before Santiago four days later and assumed charge of affairs. At that time, negotiations were going on between General Shafter and the Spanish General Toral, relative to the surrender of the latter's army and the city of Santiago. Miles at once took the matter in hand, having full authority from the Secretary of War to do so. Shafter, who had bungled the whole campaign, was afraid of being superseded and was inclined to make trouble. Eventually Miles sent him the following frank and manly telegram, which settled the matter. Miles was then at Plaza del Este:

"Have no desire and have carefully avoided any appearance of superseding you. Your command is a part of the United States Army which I have the honor to command, having been duly assigned thereto, and directed by the President to go wherever I thought my presence required, and give such general directions as I thought best concerning military matters, and especially to go to Santiago for a specific purpose.

"You will also notice that the orders of the Secretary of War, of July 13, left the matter to my discretion. I should regret that any event should cause either yourself or any part of your command to cease to be a part of mine."

The matter referred to was the surrender of General Toral, who had stated that so long as he had rations and ammunition, he would have to fight in order to maintain the honor of the Spanish army. Miles informed him that he had already done so, and that further efforts would result in the wanton sacrifice of human life. Toral surrendered, and the American forces entered Santiago on July 17. Miles did not receive the surrender himself, generously leaving that honor to Shafter. From the moment he arrived in Cuba he was charged with the responsibility of ordering an attack upon the Spanish entrenchments—which would have cost several thousand lives—or of withholding it. No greater discretion was ever given to any general commanding an army. He was also authorized to receive the surrender of the Spanish forces, but he allowed the honor to pass to another.

General Miles took charge of the army that invaded Porto Rico. The advance guard reached the port of Guanica on July 25. The campaign was brief and peculiar, the Spanish forces offering a stubborn resistance, while the inhabitants welcomed the invading army with open hands. A few days after the first landing, General Miles telegraphed the War Department in part:

" Spanish troops are retreating from southern part of Porto Rico. Ponce and port have a population of fifty thousand now under American flag. The populace received the troops and saluted the flag with wild enthusiasm. Navy has several prizes, also seventy lighters. Railway stock, partly destroyed, now restored. Telegraph communication also being restored. Cable instruments destroyed. Have sent to Jamaica for others. This is a prosperous and beautiful country. The army will soon be in the mountain region; weather delightful; troops in the best of health and spirits! anticipate no insurmountable difficulties in the future. Results thus far have been accomplished without the loss of a single life."

General Miles issued a proclamation to the people of Porto Rico, in which he assured them that "The chief aim of the American military forces will be to overthrow the authority of Spain and give the people of your beautiful island the largest measure of liberty consistent with this military occupation." Town after town surrendered to the Americans, and on August 28 General Miles informed those under his command that hostilities had been suspended. This information did not reach General Schwan until two days later, and meanwhile that officer was engaged with some Spanish forces. Upon receipt of the news, he sent a flag of truce to the enemy's line informing the officer in command that peace negotiations were nearly concluded. The Spaniard would not believe it, however, until he had communicated with the governor-general at San Juan. When he was informed from there that the information was really correct, hostilities were suspended in reality. General Miles returned to the United States and resumed his duties at Washington.

JOSEPH WHEELER.

JOSEPH WHEELER was born in Augusta, Georgia, September 10, 1836. He entered the Military Academy at West Point in 1854, and graduated four years later. He then became a lieutenant in a cavalry regiment and served in New Mexico. He cast in his fortunes with the South in the Civil War, and by his abilities rose through the different grades of the service until, in 1864, he was made the senior cavalry general of the Confederate armies. He was not only a fighter, but he was a strategist. He was audacious, aggressive, and tireless in his duties. At the age of twenty-six years, he re-

General Joseph Wheeler.

ceived the thanks of the Confederate Congress for his defence of Aiken, and the state of South Carolina honored him in the same manner for his achievements on that occasion. His services to the Confederacy were inestimable, and the name of the dashing cavalryman was known throughout the South as a household word.

Wheeler fought at Pensacola, and captured General Prentiss' brigade at Shiloh. With his gallant troopers he turned Rosecrans' flank at Murfreesboro, and at Chickamauga he was successful in capturing many prisoners, wagons and war material. After the battle, he led his swift horsemen in a famous raid around the Union rear and destroyed twelve hundred wagons loaded with supplies. He was at Missionary Ridge, and there his sabre flashed in the thickest of the fight. Later he thwarted Cook's great raid. Sixteen horses were shot under him, and he was three times wounded before the war closed.

After peace between the two warring sections had been restored, General Wheeler engaged in business in New Orleans. He declined the position of a professor and commander of cadets in the Louisiana State seminary. Instead, he became a counsellor-at-law and also a planter. Later, he was elected to Congress and served in the House of Representatives.

When the war with Spain broke out, in 1898, General Wheeler was summoned to the aid of the Government, and, in spite of his advancing years, threw himself into the conflict with the same energy he had displayed on the battlefields of the Civil War. He commanded the cavalry during the brief campaign in Cuba, and by his intelligent grasp of situations as they arose, contributed very largely to the success of the American arms. In that dismal time, when many commanders before Santiago felt

that the American forces should retreat, the grand old
cavalryman refused to entertain the proposition. The
poorly clad and worse fed heroes were almost at their last
exertion, and to some it seemed murderous to throw them
again at the Spanish defences. The monumental blunders of the campaign had brought these to feel that to
remain was disaster; to advance was extinction. "But
Wheeler had been in dilemnas of a more trying sort in the
Civil War. He had been surrounded by the bayonets of
the Federals, and many a time he had cut his way through
massive ranks that were quite as formidable as the barbed
wire bulwarks, stone walls and clay defences of the Spaniards." He wrote to the commanding officer, "I presume
the same influences are being brought to bear on you that
are working with me. But it will not do. American
prestige would suffer irretrievably if we give up an inch;
we must stand firm!"

One of the stories told of General Wheeler while in
Cuba is that, after one of the most trying battles, he ordered that trenches should be dug in anticipation of the
next conflict. Wheeler was sick at the time, but he rose
from his cot when an officer said to him:

"General, I am afraid our men can't dig the trenches."

"What men?" asked the general.

"The Cavalry Division," was the reply.

General Wheeler sat up in bed and began to pull on
his boots.

"Send me the man," he directed.

"What man?" asked the officer.

"The man who can't dig the trenches."

"But it is not one man; it is many men. They are just
played out."

" But you can surely find one man who says he can't dig the trench. Go get him and bring him to me."

After a while the officer appeared with a colored trooper.

" Are you the man who says he can't dig those trenches?"

" I'se one of them, boss, but there's a ——"

" You go to sleep now, my man, and I'll go up and dig your trench for you. When the sun comes up to-morrow morning the Spaniards are going to open on us, and every man who isn't protected will be in danger of getting killed. The trenches have to be dug, and if you are unable to dig yours, I'll just go up and dig it for you. Where's your pick?"

For a half a minute the voice of the trooper stuck in his throat, and then he said:

" Boss, you ain't fitten to dig no trenches. If they got to be dug, I'll just naturally do it myself. I'm dog tired, but that ain't no work for you."

The negro started off, and Wheeler turned to the officer saying:

" He seems to have changed his mind. Now go find me another man who can't dig the trenches."

The officer saluted and rode off. The trenches were dug before morning.

It is said that the men under him were a study and delight to General Wheeler. They moved at his will like so many machines. The fluctuating chances of battle and the scarcity of provisions at times recalled days in the Confederacy when he made campaigning very serious work for the Union armies.

After Toral's surrender, General Wheeler returned with

his men to the United States and for a time was stationed
at the camp at Montauk, Long Island.   Always a close
student, he now turned to authorship, and prepared a val-
uable work upon the operations in Cuba.   In 1899, he was
sent to the Philippine Islands to assist in the suppression
of the Filipino rebellion.

THEODORE ROOSEVELT.

THEODORE ROOSEVELT was born in New York, October 27, 1858.   He graduated from Harvard Uni-
versity in 1880, and two years later, became a member of the New York Legislature.   Later he was a National Civil Service Commissioner, and then the President of the New York Police Board.   In 1897, he was
appointed Assistant Secretary of the Navy, but resigned
from that important position in 1898, to organize the
First United States Volunteer Cavalry.

The Roosevelt family dates back to 1648, when the
Dutch were in control of Manhattan Island.   Theodore
Roosevelt's great-great-grandfather was Isaac Roosevelt,
who was a member of the Kingston Convention of 1777,
which framed the constitution of the state of New York,
and of the Poughkeepsie convention of 1786, which rati-
fied the constitution of the United States.   A son of his,
also named Isaac, was a noted inventor, and his name will
always be associated with that of Robert Fulton in the

first practical application of steam to navigation. Theodore Roosevelt's father was a prominent merchant of New
York. His brother, Robert B. Roosevelt, was at one time
minister to the Netherlands, and member of Congress.

Before his participation in the war with Spain, in 1898,
Roosevelt had been in public life for many years, and had
made a name for himself in politics and literature. He
was always active in reforms, and was successful in dis-
closing many municipal abuses in New York city. He
brought his irrepressible energies to the post of Assistant
Secretary of the Navy, and later, in speaking of his experiences in that position, said: "One day last spring,
when it fell to my lot to help get the navy ready for war,
I and my naval aide, Lieutenant Sharpe, went out buying
auxiliary cruisers. On this particular day we had spent
about seven million dollars. It began to rain. 'Sharpe,'
said I, 'I have only four cents in my pockets. Lend me
a cent or five cents, will you, so that I can ride home?'
Sharpe answered, 'I haven't a single cent.' And I answered
him, 'Never mind, Sharpe; that's why we'll beat the Spaniards. It isn't every country where two public servants
could spend seven million dollars and not have a cent in
their clothes after they were through.'"

The regiment raised by Roosevelt became known
throughout the country as the "Rough Riders." It was
composed of men from all ranks and conditions of life.
Almost in a day, Roosevelt gathered his motley throng.
The recruits came from cowboy camps and college halls,
athletes and dudes, deputy sheriffs from mining camps;
frontiersmen, men of letters, joined the ranks. Scions of
aristocratic families performed the menial duties of camp

Theodore Roosevelt.

life as gaily as they would participate in a polo match. Roosevelt declined the colonelcy of the regiment and asked that it might be given to Dr. Leonard Wood. For himself, he accepted the second command. Both he and Colonel Wood drilled the regiment until it arrived at a high state of discipline. The camp of instruction was at San Antonio, Texas, and from there the men were conveyed to Tampa, Florida, and soon sent to Cuba as dismounted cavalry.

On June 22, 1898, the "Rough Riders" disembarked from the transport Yucatan, at Daiquiri, a few miles to the eastward of Santiago, where there was an iron pier belonging to an American mining company. Getting ashore was no easy matter, as the boats were tossed about in the surf that dashed against the pier, and the soldiers were obliged to throw their rifles onto the dock, and then scramble up as best they could. On June 24, the "Rough Riders" had their first fight. Every man was eager for it, and marched gaily along. The day was swelteringly hot, and as they advanced the men threw away their blankets. They toiled on, following trails that compelled them to move in single file. Prickly cactus bushes and thick underbrush lined the way and impeded the march. Finally a little open space was reached and shots began to be heard to the right in the direction that had been taken by General Young. Shortly the crack of Mauser rifles was heard and bullets flew about the heads of the men. "It's up to us," shouted Roosevelt. Colonel Wood, as coolly as if on parade, commanded, "Deploy! lie down!" The shots came thicker and faster. The Spaniards were using smokeless powder and could not be seen.

Roosevelt braved every form of danger: men were dropping around him, and he had a narrow escape from a bullet which lodged in a tree near his head. Fourteen men were killed and thirty-six wounded before the Spaniards were located and driven back. Sergeant Hamilton Fish, Jr., was the first man killed. Captain Capron was killed while shouting an order. After the Spanish fire slackened, their troops were seen running to a blockhouse, evidently intending to make a stand there. With Roosevelt and Wood at their head the "Rough Riders" pursued them, and poured a hail of bullets into them and into the blockhouse as well. The blockhouse was abandoned when the Americans were within a few hundred yards. Its defenders fled in the direction of Santiago, and the battle of Las Guasimas was at an end.

In a letter to the Secretary of War, Colonel Wood said: " The fight lasted over two hours, and was very hot and at rather close range. The Spanish used the volley a great deal, while my men fired as individuals. We found that instead of fifteen hundred men, we had struck an outpost of several thousand. However, to cut a long story short, we drove them steadily, but slowly, and finally threw them into flight. My men conducted themselves splendidly and behaved like veterans, going up against the heavy Spanish lines as though they had the greatest contempt for them."

At El Caney, Roosevelt again showed indomitable bravery and pluck. There was no protection, the charge was in the open. A hundred feet in the lead of his men, he dashed up the slope in the face of death—men dropping at every step. Again the " Rough Riders " drove the

14

Spaniards before them, and as they fled coolly picked them off. They suffered severely, but no troops ever behaved better under fire. Colonel Wood was promoted to be a brigadier-general and Roosevelt was made a colonel. Roosevelt returned to the United States with his men and the famous regiment was mustered out of service. Roosevelt took leave of each man personally. No such body of men were ever gathered together before. Wherever stories of brave and dashing deeds are told, those of Roosevelt and his " Rough Riders " will not be omitted.

In 1899 Theodore Roosevelt was elected governor of the state of New York.

Altemus' Young People's Library.

PRICE, 50 CENTS EACH.

ROBINSON CRUSOE: His Life and Strange, Surprising Adventures. With 70 beautiful illustrations by Walter Paget.

"Was there ever anything written that the reader wished longer except ROBINSON CRUSOE and PILGRIM'S PROGRESS?"—*Samuel Johnson.*
"There exists no work, either of instruction or entertainment, which has been more generally read, and universally admired."—*Walter Scott.*

ALICE'S ADVENTURES IN WONDERLAND. With 42 illustrations by John Tenniel.

"Lewis Carroll's immortal story."—*Athenæum.*
"The most delightful of children's stories. Elegant and delicious nonsense."—*Saturday Review.*

THROUGH THE LOOKING GLASS AND WHAT ALICE FOUND THERE. (A companion to Alice in Wonderland.) With 50 illustrations by John Tenniel.

"Will fairly rank with the tale of her previous experience."—*Daily Telegraph.* . . . "Many of Tenniel's designs are masterpieces of wise absurdity."—*Athenæum.* . . . "Not a whit inferior to its predecessor in grand extravagance of imagination, and delicious allegorical nonsense." *Quarterly Review.*

BUNYAN'S PILGRIM'S PROGRESS. With 50 full-page and text illustrations.

PILGRIM'S PROGRESS is the most popular story book in the world. With the exception of the Bible it has been translated into more languages than any other book ever printed.

A CHILD'S STORY OF THE BIBLE. With 72 full-page illustrations.

Tells in simple language and in a form fitted for the hands of the younger members of the Christian flock, the tale of God's dealings with his Chosen People under the Old Dispensation, with its foreshadowings of the coming of that Messiah who was to make all mankind one fold under one Shepherd

A CHILD'S LIFE OF CHRIST. With 49 illustrations.

God has implanted in the infant's heart a desire to hear of Jesus, and children are early attracted and sweetly riveted by the wonderful Story of the Master from the Manger to the Throne.
In this little book we have brought together from Scripture every incident, expression and description, within the verge of their comprehension in the effort to weave them into a memorial garland of their Saviour.

CHRISTOPHER COLUMBUS AND THE DISCOVERY OF AMERICA. With 70 illustrations.

It is the duty of every American lad to know the story of Christopher Columbus. In this book is depicted the story of his life and struggles; of his persistent solicitations at the courts of Europe, and his contemptuous receptions by the learned Geographical Councils, until his final employment by Queen Isabella. Records the day-by-day journeyings while he was pursuing his aim and perilous way over the shoreless Ocean, until he "gave to Spain a New World." Shows his progress through Spain on the occasion of his first return, when he was received with rapturous demonstrations and more than regal homage. His displacement by the Odjeas, Ovandos and Bobadilas; his last return in chains, and the story of his death in poverty and neglect.

One distinguishing feature about this edition is, that many of the illustrations are copies from DeBry's and Herrara's histories, which were compiled by authority of the King of Spain, showing the Indians, in their life and customs, as they appeared to the early discoverers.

LIVES OF THE PRESIDENTS OF THE UNITED STATES. Compiled from authoritative sources. With portraits of the Presidents; and also of the unsuccessful candidates for the office; as well as the ablest of the Cabinet officers.

This book should be in every home and school library. It tells, in an impartial way, the story of the political history of the United States, from the first Constitutional convention till the last Presidential nominations, it is *just the book* for intelligent boys, and it will help to make them intelligent and patriotic citizens.

GULLIVER'S TRAVELS INTO SOME REMOTE REGIONS OF THE WORLD. With 50 illustrations.

In description, even of the most common-place things, his power is often perfectly marvellous. Macaulay says of SWIFT: "Under a plain garb and ungainly deportment were concealed some of the choicest gifts that ever have been bestowed on any of the children of men,—rare powers of observation, brilliant art, grotesque invention, humor of the most austere flavor, yet exquisitely delicious, eloquence singularly pure, manly, and perspicuous."

MOTHER GOOSE'S RHYMES, JINGLES, AND FAIRY TALES. With 300 illustrations.

" In this edition an excellent choice has been made from the standard fiction of the little ones. The abundant pictures are well drawn and graceful, the effect frequently striking and always decorative."—*Critic.* . . . "Only to see the book is to wish to give it to every child one knows."—*Queen.*

THE FABLES OF ÆSOP. Compiled from the best accepted sources. With 62 illustrations.

The fables of Æsop are among the very earliest compositions of this kind, and probably have never been surpassed for point and brevity, as well as for the practical good sense they display. In their grotesque grace, in their quaint humor, in their trust in the simpler virtues, in their insight int , the cruder vices, in their innocence of the fact of sex, ÆSOP'S FABLES are as little children—and for that reason they will ever find a home in the heaven of little children's souls.

THE STORY OF ADVENTURE IN THE FROZEN SEA. With 70 illustrations. Compiled from authorized sources.

We here have brought together the records of the attempts to reach the North Pole. Our object being to recall the stories of the early voyagers, and to narrate the recent efforts of gallant adventurers of various nationalities to cross the "unknown and inaccessible" threshold; and to show how much can be accomplished by indomitable pluck and steady preseverance. Portraits and numerous illustrations help the narration.
The North Polar region is the largest, as it is the most important field of discovery that remains for this generation to work out. As Frobisher declared nearly three hundred and fifty years ago, it is "the only great thing left undone in the world." Every year diminishes the extent of the unknown; and there is a bare likelihood that Dr. Nansen has already explored the hitherto unexplorable.

THE STORY OF EXPLORATION AND DISCOVERY IN AFRICA. With 80 illustrations.

Records the experiences of adventures, privations, sufferings, trials, dangers, and discoveries in developing the "Dark Continent," from the early days of Bruce and Mungo Park down to Livingstone and Stanley and the heroes of our own times.
The reader becomes carried away by conflicting emotions of wonder and sympathy, and feels compelled to pursue the story, which he cannot lay down. No present can be more acceptable than such a volume as this, where courage, intrepidity, resource and devotion are so pleasantly mingled. It is very fully illustrated with pictures worthy of the book.

THE SWISS FAMILY ROBINSON, or the Adventures of a shipwrecked Family on an Uninhabited Island. With 50 illustrations.

A remarkable tale of adventure that will interest the boys and girls. The father of the family tells the tale and the vicissitudes through which he and his wife and children pass, the wonderful discoveries they make, and the dangers they encounter. It is a standard work of adventure that has the favor of all who have read it.

THE ARABIAN NIGHTS' ENTERTAINMENTS. With 50 illustrations. Contains the most favorably known of the stories.

The text is somewhat abridged and edited for the young. It forms an excellent introduction to those immortal tales which have helped so long to keep the weary world young.

ILLUSTRATED NATURAL HISTORY. By the Rev. J. G. Wood. With 80 illustrations.

WOOD'S NATURAL HISTORY needs no commendation. Its author has done more than any other writer to popularize the study. His work is known and admired over all the civilized world. The sales of his works in England and America have been enormous. The illustrations in this edition are entirely new, striking, and life-like.

A CHILD'S HISTORY OF ENGLAND. By Charles Dickens. With 50 illustrations.

Dickens grew tired of listening to his children memorizing the old-fashioned twaddle that went under the name of English history. He thereupon wrote a book, in his own peculiarly happy style, primarily for the educational advantage of his own children, but was prevailed upon to publish the work, and make its use general. Its success was instantaneous and abiding.

BLACK BEAUTY; The Autobiography of a Horse. By Anna Sewell. With 50 illustrations.

This NEW ILLUSTRATED EDITION is sure to command attention. Wherever children are, whether boys or girls, there this Autobiography should be. It inculcates habits of kindness to all members of the animal creation. The literary merit of the book is excellent.

GRIMM'S FAIRY TALES. With 50 illustrations.

These Tales of the Brothers Grimm have carried their names into every household of the civilized world.
The Tales are a wonderful collection, as interesting, from a literary point of view, as they are delightful as stories.

ANDERSEN'S FAIRY TALES. By Hans Christian Andersen. With 77 illustrations.

The spirit of high moral teaching, and the delicacy of sentiment, feeling, and expression that pervade these tales make these wonderful creations not only attractive to the young, but equally acceptable to those of mature years, who are able to understand their real significance and appreciate the depth of their meaning.

FLOWER FABLES. By Louisa May Alcott. With colored and plain illustrations.

A series of very interesting fairy tales by the most charming of American story-tellers.

GRANDFATHER'S CHAIR; A History for Youth. By Nathaniel Hawthorne. With 60 illustrations.

The story of America from the landing of the Puritans to the *acknowledgment without reserve* of the INDEPENDENCE OF THE UNITED STATES, told with all the elegance, simplicity, grace, clearness, and force for which Hawthorne is conspicuously noted.